THE PEPPER GIRLS

Lexie & Nancy

Sandra Savage

Copyright © Sandra Savage 2015

This book is sold subject to the condition that it shall not, by way of trade or otherwise, be lent, resold, hired out, or otherwise circulated without the publisher's prior consent in any form of binding or cover other than that in which it is published and without a similar condition including this condition being imposed on the subsequent publisher.

The moral right of Sandra Savage has been asserted

Dedicated to my lovely grandson John McGlashan IV, as he likes to be known.

This is a work of fiction. Names, characters, businesses, organizations, places, events and incidents either are the product of the author's imagination or are used fictitiously. Any resemblance to actual persons, living or dead, events, or locales is entirely coincidental.

CONTENTS

Chapter 1 .... *1*
Chapter 2 .... *6*
Chapter 3 .... *10*
Chapter 4 .... *16*
Chapter 5 .... *21*
Chapter 6 .... *26*
Chapter 7 .... *30*
Chapter 8 .... *35*
Chapter 9 .... *39*
Chapter 10 .... *44*
Chapter 11 .... *49*
Chapter 12 .... *53*
Chapter 13 .... *57*
Chapter 14 .... *63*
Chapter 15 .... *67*
Chapter 16 .... *71*
Chapter 17 .... *75*
Chapter 18 .... *81*
Chapter 19 .... *85*
Chapter 20 .... *91*
Chapter 21 .... *95*
Chapter 22 .... *98*
Chapter 23 .... *102*
Chapter 24 .... *106*
Chapter 25 .... *112*
Chapter 26 .... *116*

Chapter 1

Life for Lexie was wonderful. She had achieved the grand position of Senior Typist at Baxters, and at the age of seventeen, just turned, was 'going steady' with Charlie Mathieson, a recently qualified Draughtsman who worked in the Drawing Office at Verdant Works, a jute mill off Blackness Road, or the 'Blackie' as it was known in Dundee.

Yes, Annie MacPherson's daughter had done well for herself and that weekend, unknown to her mother and step-father, she and Charlie were going into town to start shopping for her engagement ring.

But, for Lexie's mother, things couldn't have been more different.

"Do you think Lexie's alright?" Annie asked her husband Euan MacPherson for the umpteenth time, keenly aware of the letter she had received from Belfast two weeks ago with some unexpected news, which she wished she could share with Euan, but dare not.

Euan held up his finger to his lips. "Sssshhh, now Annie, you know you're getting a terrible worrier of late and if only half the things you worried about happened, we'd be living on the streets by now."

Annie busied herself with her knitting. "I know, I know," she said, "but it's just that she rushes into things without a thought for the consequences and then, well, who knows what's ahead of her..."

Annie's voice tapered off, keenly aware that she was recognising herself in the statement as well as her daughter.

The slamming of the front door signalled the arrival of Ian, Annie and Euan's young son, who had progressed to the 'big school' and was now in his second year at the Morgan, situated on Forfar Road, not far from their home in Albert Street.

"What's for tea?" he called, rummaging in the kitchen cupboards to find some of his mother's baking to 'keep him going' till then. Ian was fast leaving boyhood behind him and at fourteen could hold his own with the fastest runners and best football players in his class. Academically, he could 'try harder' as his school reports frequently said, but Euan was happy with his son's progress and had already decided his future would be in the police force, although Ian was unaware of this and had sweet dreams of becoming a football player and playing for Dundee.

"Hi dad," he beamed, as he kissed Annie fleetingly on the top of her head, "I've only been picked for the school team," he grinned. "Centre Forward too," he added, "Mr McGregor says I've got the height and the heart," he added proudly. He finished off the sultana scone he'd found in the cake tin, smacking his lips and settling down beside Annie on the sofa.

"Tea's at six o'clock," his mother told him, "your dad's shift starts at eight and Lexie should be home soon, so just get on with your homework and I'll get started on the cooking."

Glad of the chance to escape to the solitude of the kitchen, Annie packed away her knitting and headed for the parlour door.

She knew she was worrying too much about Lexie but the reason for her disquiet was the contents of the latest letter she'd received from Ireland and the effect it could have on the bond she had with her daughter.

Euan lit his pipe and unfolded his newspaper. Annie was a wonderful wife and mother, he assured himself and since the christening of Nancy and Billy Donnelly's little girl, Mary Anne, two years since, she seemed to have become even more contented, until recently that is.

There was a while back then, when he'd wondered about Annie and her first love, the obsessive Billy Dawson. She had received a mysterious letter from Ireland at that time and, despite asking on several occasions to see the letter, she had never been forthcoming and he had eventually let it drop. But now and then, when Annie seemed lost in her own thoughts, he would wonder again about that letter.

The Smokies were heating nicely in the oven and the delicious smell of smoked fish and butter was wafting through the kitchen, when Lexie breezed in, wearing her kid gloves, as usual. Essential for a Senior Typist, Mrs Fyffe had told her, to keep her hands protected from the elements. She screwed up her nose at the strong smell.

"Friday at last," she said, draping her coat over a chair and dropping her gloves and handbag on the dresser.

"It may be Friday," Annie echoed, "but there's a place for everything and everything in its place," she nodded towards the dresser, "and that's not the place for a handbag and gloves."

Lexie smiled, picking up the offending items and sweeping her coat over her arm. "OK," she said sweetly, taking them through to her room before returning and offering to help her mother.

"You can set the table," Annie told her, "and while you're doing that, you can tell me about your day."

"The day's been fine," Lexie began, "but it's tomorrow that's going to be exciting."

Annie stopped mashing the potatoes. "Oh!" she exclaimed, "and what's so special about tomorrow?"

"TOMORROW," Lexie emphasised, "Charlie and me are going into town to look at engagement rings." She wiggled the third finger of her left hand in front of her mother. "He asked me to marry him on my birthday last week and I said YES."

Lexie clasped her hands together and gazed into nowhere as she relived the moment in her mind's eye.

"Isn't it wonderful?" she said, finally focussing on her mother's less than pleased expression.

"What's wrong?" she asked, suddenly sensing the change in atmosphere.

This was the last thing Annie had expected to hear and her spirits plummeted. How could Lexie take such a huge decision without telling her first and especially now! Annie's son, born out of wedlock in the poorhouse in Belfast and fathered by Billy Dawson was soon to be on his way to Dundee and wanting to meet Annie and maybe her family for the first time.

Annie's son, John, had been adopted at birth by a Belfast doctor and his wife. The nuns had spared no time in arranging the adoption, while Annie had sunk into a deep depression, saved only by the gentle care from her fellow-inmate, Bella, who had looked after her and who Annie had left behind when she came to Scotland.

"Weren't you engaged once before," Annie reminded her, her voice more forceful than she intended, "to Robbie Robertson, wasn't it and we all know how that ended, your father having to warn him off because you'd 'changed your mind' after two weeks."

Lexie flinched. "But, I was only fifteen then," she squealed and needed no reminder of the real reason she had 'changed her mind' but that was a secret no one, not even Charlie knew about.

"I'm seventeen now and Charlie and me are in love," she told Annie loudly, hurt and confused at her mother's disapproval.

"I thought you liked Charlie," she said, "you always said you liked him."

Euan came into the kitchen, followed hard on his heels by Ian.

"What's all the noise," Euan asked, quickly realising that mother and daughter were at loggerheads again.

Lexie burst into tears. "Mum hates Charlie," she sobbed, "but I love him and we're getting married..." her red eyes glared at her mother, "whether you like it or not," she added as she ran from the room.

Ian grinned and looked from one parent to the other. He loved a good fight and this one was shaping up to be a 'biggie.'

Annie flopped down on a chair and pulled her apron up over her face, trying to mask the fear she felt for her daughter, herself and the future.

Ian stopped grinning, realising it was more serious than the usual spats Lexie had with her mother. "I'll get on with my homework then," he mumbled, inching his way out of the kitchen but not before retrieving another scone from the cake tin.

Euan pulled up a chair beside Annie. "Hey," he said gently, lifting the apron from her eyes, "what's this all about," he urged, "you can tell me anything, you know that."

Annie sighed and shook her head. "She's just too young," she whispered, making Lexie's age the focus of her fear. "And what kind of a future will there be for them in Dundee," she continued, "the mills are on short time, they say there's a recession on the way and what will become of them if she..." Annie hesitated.

"If she what?" asked Euan.

She turned tearful eyes on her husband, "What if she gets pregnant... like Nancy did, what then!"

Euan put his arm around her shoulder and pulled her into him.

"I've told you before, you worry too much," he said, his words heavy with resignation, "but I see what you mean," he conceded with a sigh. "Maybe if I have a word with Charlie, see what he thinks, would that help?"

Annie nodded. "Maybe," she said, painfully aware that she was stalling. Euan of all people needed to know the truth about Billy Dawson's son, but not now, not till the time was right, if ever that arrived. The first letter from her son John's adopted parents had been a shock, but over the two years since then, she had formed a wonderful bond with her son, writing to him regularly while praying for the right time to broach the subject with Euan and her family, but panic always overwhelmed her.

But now, it looked like fate was making the decision for her. Her illegitimate son, John Adams, who was a medical student in Belfast was coming to Dundee on an Exchange Scholarship for six months and couldn't wait to meet her in person.

Euan patting her gently, brought her back into the moment.

"Now, how about those Smokies," he soothed, trying for normality and failing, "they smell lovely. You dish them out and I'll calm Lexie down."

Annie held Euan's arm. "It's a changing world," she said, "and it's women who are having to change the most. She's not worldly wise like Nancy and if anything happened to her, to hurt her, I don't think I could bear it."

Annie remembered her daughter's reaction to Nancy's unplanned pregnancy with Billy Donnelly and the hastily arranged wedding. Lexie had been horrified and ashamed by it all. And now, to find out her own mother was a 'fallen woman' with a bastard son was too much for Annie to cope with. Lexie would never understand, not at her young age and she could end up losing her forever, especially if she got married and left home. Euan gathered her into his arms. "Nothing's going to happen to her Annie," he assured her, still trying to grasp why his wife seemed so anxious, "not while I'm around."

But Annie wasn't so sure.

Chapter 2

Annie's niece, Nancy had set up home with Billy Donnelly and their little girl Mary Anne, in one of the grey stone tenements in Lochee, built by the mill owners to house their workers. Billy was a well-liked spinner at Cox's Mill and the Manager, Mr McKay, had spoken up for him and his need for housing, when Nancy and him had wed, 'albeit rather quickly' as he'd put it to the Mill Factor.

"Daddy will be home soon," she cooed to Mary Anne, in an attempt to stop her wriggling and wanting to explore everything with her tiny toddler fingers. There was always so much to do, Nancy mused, as she looked around the cramped kitchen, the sideboard and table pushed together to make room for Mary Anne's cot.

The birth of her daughter had been difficult, but Billy's Catholic upbringing, despite the fact that he'd been excommunicated on marrying her, still meant that any form of birth control was out of the question.

She patted her swollen stomach. Where they were going to fit another child into the tiny space, let alone find the money to feed another mouth filled her with dread. Married life and having babies hadn't been her idea of how life would be, but like the other women around her, it seemed to be her lot. 'She'd made her bed, now she'd have to lie in it,' was the stock answer to any complaint she voiced about the unfairness of it all and that, along with the directive that 'hard work never killed anybody' left her in no illusion that things were going to change any time soon, whether she liked it or not. This was definitely how life was always going to be.

The sound of her husband's footsteps coming up the stairwell roused her into action. "C'mon Mary Anne," she said, sweeping the child into her arms and depositing her in her cot. "Daddy's home now, so be a good girl and let mammy get on with his tea."

Billy Donnelly came into his home, bringing with him the overwhelming aroma of jute which clung to his clothes and hair. For him too, life hadn't worked out quite as he'd expected. He'd had dreams of travelling all over the Highlands and Islands and even working a small croft, far away from the industrial lowlands where he was rooted. But getting Nancy pregnant had changed all that and now, with another mite on the way, any thoughts of going anywhere but to Cox's Mill and back home again had been consigned to the dustbin.

"Good day?" he asked Nancy as he crossed the room to Mary Anne's cot, tickling her under the chin and getting her agitated again.

"For goodness sake Billy, leave her alone," Nancy chided, "she's needing a sleep and I've the tea to get ready..." She pushed past Billy impatiently and hushed the baby while Billy retreated to his chair by the hearth and threw some more coal on the fire to get a blaze going.

"I'm sorry," Nancy muttered, glancing at her crestfallen husband, "it's been a long day and this baby of yours has been moving like it's wanting to be born right now, not in six weeks' time."

Billy hung his head, "I'm sorry too," he said, indicating for her to sit down. "I've some news," he began, "and it's not good."

Nancy sat down, folded her hands in her lap and waited.

"The mill's going on short-time from next week," he said, "the work's drying up and it's either that or layoffs."

Nancy felt her mouth go dry. "What does that mean for us?" she asked, now fearful of his reply.

"It means that I'll only be working and getting paid for three days work a week."

Nancy could feel the fear creeping through her entire body.

"Half-wages," she whispered, "but we barely manage on full pay Billy and with a second baby on the way..." the reality of what she was saying silenced her.

"This isn't my choice Nancy," Billy told her, anger now beginning to build at the unfairness of their life, "but it's all we've got, so let's just get on with it." He picked up his recently discarded jacket. "I need to walk," he said, heading for the door, "clear my mind. I'm sorry." The door slammed.

Nancy had never felt so alone as the silence enveloped her, nor so helpless at their plight. That night she prayed fervently for help to arrive but the next day, the only thing that arrived were the beginnings of her labour pains.

Billy had come home late and gone to work early when the twinges she had felt during the night suddenly escalated. Her 'waters broke' and a searing pain clamped around her womb. She staggered outside, barely able to stand, and hammered as loudly as she could on her neighbour's door.

"Whit's up," came the bleary voice of Nan Duncan as she peered round the door, her hair in curlers and her flannel nightgown clasped at her chest.

"The baby," Nancy gasped, "it's coming!"

"Oh, my Goad!" Nan said, panic rising in her voice, "Rab," she shouted into the kitchen, "get Dr Finlayson," she ordered her husband, "Nancy's bairn's on the way."

"C'mon," she urged Nancy, "let's get you to bed." Slowly and painfully, the women returned to Nancy's home.

"Rab'll ha'e the doctor here soon," she told Nancy, trying to bring reassurance into her voice, "jist haud on lassie."

Dr Finlayson, a shrunken man carrying his black doctor's bag, hurried in an hour later and took charge.

"The baby's crowning," he stated, "it won't be long now."

The force of the baby's push to be born was weak, but with Dr Finlayson's encouragement, Nancy pushed with all her might, till she felt the squelch of her child slithering into the world.

The kitchen door banged open and Billy Donnelly rushed in.

"Nancy," he called, hurrying to her side, "I didn't know," he whispered tearfully, "Rab came and got me. Why didn't you say something?" He looked at the tiny form barely moving and at the doctor. "Is everything alright," he asked anxiously, "it wasn't expected this soon." The doctor ignored him and continued to focus on Nancy and her newborn. He picked up the new life and slapped it on its backside. There was a juddering in the child's body as it tried to breath. He slapped it again, as Nancy and Billy stared in horror. Just then, a broken cry could be heard as Nancy's tiny son took his first breath.

"There now," Dr Finlayson murmured wrapping the child in a clean towel. "Cry all you want, young man, those little lungs of yours need exercising." He turned to Nan Duncan, "maybe a cup of tea would be in order for mother," he instructed, "while we get her and baby tidied up."

He finally handed the baby to Billy. "That was a close call," he said quietly, "let's hope the baby thrives and makes up for his shaky start."

Billy nodded. "And Mr Donnelly," the doctor continued, "I think you need to make a decision as to what you want." Billy looked confused.

He drew him aside while Nan Duncan handed Nancy her tea.

"Two births, this close together have taken their toll on your wife and another might finish her, so make up your mind which you'd rather have, your wife or your Catholic religion, if you get my meaning." He looked over at Nancy, "I know which one I'd choose."

Once again, his Catholic faith had brought Billy nothing but anguish.

"Thanks doctor," he said, "I understand." Memories of the priest telling him that God wanted his flock of good Catholics to increase and it was every man's duty to make sure this happened filled his head.

"If you'll let me know how much we're owed," he murmured shakily, "I'll pay it as soon as I can."

The doctor nodded sagely, patting the young man on the shoulder, knowing that it may be a long time before he'd be paid. "When you can," he said, "when you can."

Nan Duncan took Mary Anne back to her own home to look after her till Nancy got some rest. "Let me know if there's onythin' else I can do," she offered. "I'll bring some bread and milk through in a while if that's a'right."

Billy nodded. Never had he been so glad of anyone as he had been that day of Nan Duncan and things were going to be different now, he vowed, he didn't know how he was going to do it, but he was going to find enough money to feed his wife and family. He had a son now, and no son of his was going to starve or end up working in a jute mill all his life.

He pushed the towel gently away from his son's face. His skin was redder now and his cry was getting louder and more insistent. "I think he's looking for his tea," Nancy whispered, reaching for the child before undoing her nightgown and guiding the tiny mouth towards her nipple. With a soft tug, the baby began to suck.

Billy stroked Nancy's hair, "Everything's going to alright now," he told her, "I'm going to make sure of it." Nancy nodded, the Billy she'd fallen in love with was back. Poverty and life had driven a wedge between them for a while, but their new son had brought them back together again and hope filled Nancy's heart once more.

Chapter 3

The atmosphere in the MacPherson household was decidedly frosty as Annie scrambled the eggs for their Saturday breakfast. Despite Euan's attempts at brokering a reconciliation between mother and daughter, Lexie had taken to her room where she remained, silent and aloof.

Euan sat at the kitchen table, smoking his pipe and pretending to read yesterday's newspaper, while waiting for Ian and Lexie to rush in, as usual, eager to start the weekend, but only Ian arrived, a perplexed look on his face at his sister's absence.

Annie dished out the eggs and toast while Euan attempted, once more, to bring the situation back to normal.

"Lexie's sleeping late," he stated, glancing at the kitchen clock.

Annie nodded agreement. "Looks like it."

Ian forked huge mouthfuls of scrambled eggs followed by slices of buttered toast.

"If Lexie's not having any breakfast, can I have hers?" he asked, hopefully, his demanding appetite winning over his manners.

"No, you can't," said Euan, emphatically, "Lexie will be through shortly, so just finish your own and leave the table."

Ian shrugged and fell into clearing his plate.

Annie had barely touched her eggs, but nibbled, birdlike, on a piece of toast her stomach knotted so tightly at the thought of the confrontation she anticipated with Lexie, that nothing would go down.

She picked up the teapot to refill it when the kitchen door opened and Lexie entered, her eyes red-rimmed and her mouth set in a determined line.

Ian started to giggle at Lexie's puffy face, but soon stopped as his sister turned a doleful gaze in his direction.

"Isn't it time for your football practice?" Euan asked his son, breaking the ice that was rapidly filling the kitchen. Sons were so uncomplicated, he thought, but daughters, well they were fast getting beyond his comprehension, especially Lexie.

Glad of an excuse to leave the table, Ian grabbed another piece of toast and nodded quizzically to his dad. It was only half past eight and football didn't start till gone ten! "Come on," Euan said, rising from the table, "I'll help you polish your boots," he too, glad of any excuse to leave the kitchen.

Wordlessly, Annie set the plate of eggs before Lexie and poured herself some tea. The plate was pushed aside and the 'battle of wills' that Annie had been dreading began.

"Not hungry?" she asked quietly.

Lexie shook her head, her chin already quivering with hurt at her mother.

"I'm sorry about what I said," Annie continued, "about Robbie Robertson, I mean, but maybe you can understand that I'm only worried about you and your future."

Lexie's voice quivered. "Well," she said quietly, "you won't have to worry about me much longer. Charlie and me are getting engaged and married and the quicker the better as far as I'm concerned, then I'll be gone out of here... FOREVER," she added defiantly.

Annie's worst fear was realized and the dam of tears that she'd been holding inside suddenly broke and poured unchecked down her face.

The shock of seeing her mother in this state frightened Lexie into action and pushing her chair back she rushed to her mother's side.

She loved her mother very much and hated that her announcement had caused such distress, but she did love Charlie Mathieson too and in her young mind, that was all that mattered.

Mother and daughter held onto one another till all tears ceased, both realising that none of them wanted to lose the other, but knowing that something had to change.

Tea was made and drank quietly. Was now the time to tell Lexie about her half-brother in Belfast, Annie pondered, but almost instantly rejected the idea. The one who needed to know was Billy Dawson, this was his doing and Annie hated that the past continued to haunt her.

"You know I love you very much," she said to Lexie, who nodded silently, "and you know that I wish only happiness for you..."

"I know," Lexie interrupted, "and I love you too mammy, but..."

It was Annie's turn to quieten the other.

"I know you love Charlie and that it's important to you that you get engaged and be married." Lexie brightened. Her mother was seeing reason at last.

"But," continued Annie, "all I ask is that you wait for a year, one year only till you're eighteen before you get engaged."

Lexie hadn't expected this.

"But, WHY?" she wailed, her selfish side re-emerging, "what difference will that make?"

Annie took her daughter's hands in hers. She needed to use all her powers of persuasion to buy the six months of time she needed for her son's visit to Dundee to come and go, with the dangers of exposure that involved. Once he'd gone, things would go back to letter writing and no one would need to know anything about her past, especially not her daughter.

"The world's changing Lexie," she began, "and unless I'm mistaken there's not going to be much work around for anyone in Dundee soon and that includes Charlie and yourself. If you'd become a Dundee weaver like you'd wanted, you'd have been paid off by now. The mills are on short-time all over town, and how would you manage then, with a home to run and maybe a family on the way and no money coming in..."

Annie tried to paint as black a picture as she could and it seemed to be working.

Lexie sighed audibly. "So, you think things will be better next year?" she asked naively.

"I do," Annie lied, squeezing her daughter's hand tighter.

"I'll speak to Charlie when I see him later," she conceded, secretly hoping that he would want to throw caution to the wind and they'd run away together and get married before anyone could stop them.

But while Annie was reasoning with Lexie, Euan was paying an early morning visit to Charlie Mathieson.

"Mr MacPherson!" Charlie exclaimed, "I wasn't expecting to see you. Come on in and I'll get mum to make you some tea."

"No thanks," said Euan, "I just need a few words with yourself."

Charlie looked Euan squarely in the face. "She's told you, hasn't she," he stated.

Euan nodded. "She has, Charlie," he said, "and her mother's not very happy about it, what with Lexie being so young and all and the mills laying workers off…" Euan let the thought hang in the air between them. At twenty years of age, Charlie was much more worldly-wise than Lexie and had already heard rumours that the Verdant Mill was considering short-time for its spinners and weavers and secretly doubting his decision to get engaged right now. But Lexie was so beautiful and he just wanted her for his own before anyone else could come along and impress her more.

Charlie ran his fingers through his hair. "Aye, it's a bad business all round," he agreed, "but I've already asked Lexie to marry me and she's said yes, so…"

Euan smiled, he was warming to Charlie Mathieson more and more.

"I can see you're a sensible young man Charlie," he told him, "and we don't have a problem with you and Lexie getting married, just not quite yet, that's all."

Charlie looked at his watch. "We're meeting at one o'clock outside Hendersons Jewellers, maybe then I'll have thought of a way to tell her the engagement is off, for the moment at least." He looked at Euan, worry creasing his young face. "She'll not be pleased," he said anxiously.

"No, she won't," Euan agreed, "but it would be worse if you got married then lost your job, surely."

The two men shook hands. "Leave it with me," Charlie told him unsteadily, "and wish me luck."

Neither Charlie nor Lexie were now looking forward to their meeting but when he saw her coming towards him as he waited outside the jewellers, all thoughts of putting things off were pushed aside by his desire for her.

The jangling of the shop doorbell announced their entrance.

Silently, but for the ticking of a grandmother clock which stood in the corner, the couple approached the counter and gazed at the display of sparking rings under the glass.

"Can I be of help?" asked a quiet voice.

Charlie and Lexie jumped. "We didn't hear you come through from the back," Charlie stuttered, "sorry."

Mr Henderson smiled. "Not very busy today," he said, "but I'm sure things will pick up before too long." He inclined his head towards Charlie, "and what can we do for you, Sir?"

"We're looking for an engagement ring," he said, encircling Lexie with a protective arm.

Mr Henderson raised his eyebrows slightly. "Engagement ring, you say, well, as you can see," he advised them, indicating the trays of rings before them, "we've quite a lot to choose from."

Lexie was entranced by the colours in the diamonds being reflected by the overhead lights. How she longed to have one on her finger.

"Does Sir have a price range in mind?" he asked Charlie in a loud whisper.

Euan's words returned uninvited into his mind about losing his job and he annoyingly remembered he was meant to be delaying the engagement, not encouraging it.

"Can't afford too much," he said loudly, "not with the way things are at Verdant Works."

Lexie flinched. Her mother was right then and now Charlie was saying the same thing. Times were hard and going to get harder.

She turned her attention to the tray of rings priced at £4.10/- "I'll have one of those," she said stoutly, "that one," she added, pointing out a silver ring with a single semi-precious stone set in a claw.

The jeweller gingerly removed the ring from the tray for Lexie to try on. She slipped it on the third finger of her left hand.

"There," she said to an embarrassed Charlie, who'd been prepared to spend at least £10 on Lexie's ring, "this will do nicely."

The jeweller sniffed. "Will that be all?" he asked Charlie drily.

With a quick nod, he paid for the ring and waited impatiently till it had been placed in a small box and handed over to him.

"I hope you'll both be very happy," the jeweller intoned, "very happy."

Charlie rushed Lexie out of the shop. This wasn't how it was meant to be at all, none of it and all the joy he'd felt at Lexie's acceptance of his proposal, seemed to diminish in worth to the size of the cheap ring.

"We need a cup of tea," he said hoarsely, guiding Lexie across the road to a small hotel at the top of Castle Street, "let's go in here," he said, "we need to talk."

He ordered tea for two and after the waitress had deposited the tray of cups, saucers and silver tea service on their table, Charlie pulled his chair closer to Lexie.

"That's not an engagement ring you've chosen," he told her, "it's just a cheap piece of jewellery that means nothing."

Lexie smiled to herself. "It means more to me than any expensive ring," she said, "because it's only temporary."

"Temporary!" exclaimed Charlie, "what do you mean, temporary?"

Lexie braced herself and explained about the conservation she'd had with her mother and that they would be selfish to get engaged right now, with work being the way it was and everyone worried about the future.

"So," she continued, "I don't think we should get engaged till next year, when I'm eighteen, but until then, this ring will be a token of that future promise and I shall wear it till then, only I'll wear it on a chain around my neck and not on my finger. That will be kept free till we really get engaged with a proper diamond ring."

Charlie sat back in amazement. "What a wonderful idea," he said, grinning from ear to ear, "it'll be our secret for now and when the time is right, we can tell everyone the truth."

Charlie had a slight feeling of having been manipulated by Annie and Euan, but also knew deep down in his heart, that they could be right about the unemployment that was now creeping into the mills and the looks on the faces of people on the streets as they were forced to live on less and less money.

The relief that flooded Annie's soul when Charlie and Lexie told her that they'd postponed their engagement for a year was overwhelming and Euan too felt the tension ease as he hugged his daughter and shook Charlie's hand.

"I'm sure you've made the right decision," he said solemnly, "and let's hope that by this time next year, the future is rosier for us all."

Annie hated coercing Euan unknowingly into helping her keep the balance of her household intact for now, but she vowed that as soon as her son returned to Ireland, she would tell her husband everything.

Chapter 4

It was early on Sunday morning when Billy Donnelly knocked on Billy Dawson's door. Wee Billy was four weeks old now and beginning to gain weight, not a lot, but enough for Nancy to stop fretting over him so much.

He reasoned that Billy Dawson should know that he was a grandfather again, albeit sooner than was expected, but he also wanted to sound him out about work at Baxters.

Cox's Mill was now talking about laying workers off, so even the half-time pay he was earning at the moment may soon turn into nothing at all.

Billy Dawson was surprised to see his son-in-law standing on the doorstep and immediately thought something was wrong with Nancy or Mary Anne.

"Billy!" he exclaimed, searching the young man's face for assurance that all was well. "Nothing wrong I hope?"

Billy took off his bonnet and began to run his fingers nervously round the rim. "No, Mr Dawson, nothing's wrong," he said, "in fact, I'm here to tell you some good news."

Billy breathed a sigh of relief, "Well, in that case," he smiled, "come away in."

"Look who's here," he called into the kitchen to Josie and his daughters who were enjoying their Sunday breakfast.

Billy popped his head round the door. "Mornin' Missus," he said, nodding first to Josie and then to the three girls in turn.

Josie's first reaction was also that something was wrong but was soon reassured. "Billy's got some good news," announced her husband, "and as soon as you've given him a cup of tea and some toast, he'll tell us all about it, isn't that right Billy?"

Space was made for him at the table, Sarah fetched a cup and saucer and plate for him as Josie boiled some water for more tea.

"Tea won't be a moment," she told him, "help yourself to the toast and there's some raspberry jam there, if you fancy it."

Billy couldn't help comparing his own home with the one he was now in. Sure, Nancy did her best with the money they had, but there wasn't much could be done to improve the dingy hovel that was home and any food they had went first to himself to keep his strength up for working and then Mary Anne, often leaving very little for Nancy. Dr Finlayson had been right, another pregnancy would probably kill his wife, so he did the only thing he could to meet the demands of his faith and that was, abstention. Nancy was always too tired at night for any loving anyway, but for Billy, it was turning into deep frustration.

"Thanks Missus," he said, "tea will be fine, I've already eaten."

Josie glanced at her husband in disbelief. Billy Donnelly was gaunt of feature and pale skinned. "Well, no bother," she said, "I'll put a few things into a basket for you to take home to Nancy and Mary Anne, it'll save her shopping for a bit," and before he could protest she poured his tea, spooning three lots of sugar into it for him.

"So," began Billy, "what's this good news you've got?"

"You're a grandpa again," he announced firmly, "me and Nancy have a new bairn, a boy, little Billy."

There was a stunned silence. They knew that Nancy was pregnant again, Annie had met Josie out shopping and told her the news.

"But, surely, she's not due for a while yet?" queried Josie.

Billy shrugged. "The little mite couldn't wait to be born, so turned up early."

Josie looked to her husband with concern in her eyes.

"And is everything fine, the bairn and Nancy...?"

"Getting better every day," he bluffed, "we're all 'in the pink' as they say."

"Does that mean I'm an Auntie," asked Jane, Josie's youngest to no one in particular.

Sarah nudged her to hush up, aware that her mother wasn't sure about how happy the announcement of the new arrival actually was.

Billy Dawson hadn't said much, but was picking up on his wife's concerns, so when she suggested the two men go through to the parlour for a comfortable sit down, he didn't object.

"We'll just get the dishes done and make up that basket," she smiled, indicating to her daughters to start the clearing up.

Once out of earshot of the women, Billy's facade of happiness faltered.

"I'm sorry, Mr Dawson," he murmured, "I'm happy to have a son, but with two hungry mouths to feed now and Cox's on short time, with maybe worse to come, I've also come to beg you for help."

Billy could see the shame and distress that was folding about his son-in-law and his anger at the unfairness of his plight tightened his innards.

"You don't have to beg son," he said, his voice barely above a whisper, "there's no shame in poverty, only grief."

Tears were glittering in Billy's eyes as he looked at the young man in front of him, whose only 'crime' had been to love his daughter, and the consequences of that had now brought him to this point.

"What can I do to help?" he asked simply.

"Work, Mr Dawson," he said, desperately, "I need work. I'm a good spinner and hard worker and if there's any way you can find a job for me at Baxters, maybe..." He ran out of words and his head tipped forward shaking from side to side.

Billy watched the young man in silence. He knew more than anyone how many mills were on short time and in Dundee there weren't many alternatives out there for employment.

Baxters had been one of the lucky ones. They had won government contracts for hessian sacking and sailcloth, which would last them through the coming year but, even here, cutting the workforce was being considered.

"Leave it with me," he finally said, "I won't see you and Nancy and the bairns go hungry." Billy raised his eyes to meet those of his saviour.

"You mean..."

"I mean," said Billy, "I'll do my best to get you work at Baxters, full-time too, but it may not be at the spinning, it may be in the Batching House or as a Stower's Labourer at one of the warehouses, but it'll be work and it'll keep the wolf from the door." Billy was speechless, at last, he could see a way forward thanks to Nancy's father and he'd never forget his kindness, he vowed, not if he lived to be a hundred.

"Now, off you go back home to wee Billy and I'll get word to you through Mr MacKay at Cox's."

The young man's shoulders straightened and still unable to speak without breaking down, he nodded his thanks to Billy.

"And, don't forget the basket Josie's making up for Nancy," he added thankful that he was in a position to help his daughter and her family who had so little, when he had so much.

But, this wasn't always the case, when he'd come back from the war, shell-shocked and broken, there had been kindness shown to him by Isabella and John Anderson, the Salvationists and Annie Pepper herself who had knitted socks as part of the war effort and, unknown to her, they had reached him at the field hospital at Ypres and gave him the strength to keep going. He shook the memories from his mind and followed Billy to the door, now bearing the basket of food Josie had prepared for him.

"Say hello to Nancy from me," he said, "I'll come and see you all soon... and Billy..." he reached into his pocket and produced two half-crowns. "That's for wee Billy from his Grandad."

Speechless again, Billy brushed a tear from his eye and went home to his wife and family.

Nancy couldn't believe her eyes when she lifted the cloth covering the basket that Billy had brought back with him. There were eggs, butter, cheese, bread, potatoes, oatmeal and a jar of raspberry jam, all nestling on a chequered cloth.

She turned amazed eyes to Billy, "But where...?"

Billy took a deep breath. "I've been to see your dad to tell him about wee Billy and, Nancy, he's going to get me work at Baxters. Full-time work too, so you don't have to worry anymore." Tears blurred her eyes as she looked at her husband and the wonderful basket of food.

She had been near to breaking point, with little nourishment and the bairn sucking the goodness out of her at every feed.

"And he gave me this." Billy produced the two silver coins from his pocket. "They're for wee Billy, so you can buy him the things he needs now." He handed the money over to Nancy, who was the one who was now speechless. Billy Dawson may not have been there for her when she was growing up and her mother, Mary, was alive, but he had made up for it ever since, paying for Mary Anne's christening and looking out for her and

Billy when Joe Cassiday's obsession had forced her to leave home and now this.

Billy hugged her for the first time in many weeks and he could feel her softness and warmth awakening the desire in him. He gently pushed her away. "So, let's have a feast," he said, "everything's going to be alright now."

But for Billy, nothing was going to alright again.

Chapter 5

Lexie strung her ring onto a silver chain and fastened it around her neck. She looked at herself in the mirror, in a year from now, she decided, she'd be getting married, not engaged, as her mother believed, because after all, she was engaged already, albeit secretly.

She skipped through to the kitchen where Annie was ironing Euan's shirts. The flat iron had been heating on the gas ring and carefully Annie lifted it onto the table where she tested it on a folded towel to make sure it wasn't too hot. Lexie stood fascinated. "Will you show me how to do that," she asked, "so that I can iron Charlie's shirts when we're married?"

Annie glanced at her daughter. "You won't be needing to know how to iron for a long time yet, so enjoy your leisure while you can, there'll be plenty time for domestic duties when you have to do them." Annie pushed the iron over the collar and cuffs of the stiff cotton shirt and hoped that Lexie would change the subject. But Lexie just shrugged and announced that Charlie and her were going to the new cinema that had opened in Bank Street, the Kinnaird it was called, and she'd not be home late, but not to wait up.

Annie finished her ironing and re-read John's letter over a cup of tea.

Dear Annie

I've got some great news. The Faculty of Medicine have arranged for an Exchange Scholarship with a student from the Medical School in Dundee. I didn't think I'd stand a chance of getting it, but it must have been my lucky day, so you and I will be able to meet face to face at last.

The exchange lasts for six months and I'll be working at the Dundee Royal Infirmary and lodging at a boarding house in Union Street from 1st March till the end of the term in August.

I'll be in touch nearer the time and I can't wait to meet you and, hopefully, some of your family, if that's possible.

Yours impatiently,

John

Annie folded the letter carefully and returned it to her apron pocket.

She longed to see her son, but the fear of the consequences that this meeting would bring if it were to become known to Lexie and Euan for that matter, didn't bear thinking about.

As for Billy Dawson, she had decided that he would never be revealed as the father, to either his son nor Josie and the girls.

No, better the identity of John's father never be known, not ever.

Annie was transferring the ironed clothes to the airing cupboard when Euan came in. He'd been on an early shift and it had only just gone half past two.

"You look a bit hot and bothered," he said as he kissed Annie on the cheek and took in the neatly ironed shirts folded on the shelves. "How about I take you out for a nice walk in the fresh air?"

Annie looked out of the window, "Well, I suppose Ian won't be home for a couple of hours yet and I've spent the last three hours ironing..."

"So, that's a yes, then," Euan said, fetching her coat and hat from the hallstand.

Annie smiled. "That's a definite yes." How kind and considerate he was, she thought, always making sure she was happy and contented and being a wonderful father to Lexie and Ian. How could she possibly tell him about her past, even if she kept Billy Dawson's name out of it, what she had done was shameful and no amount of time passing was altering that.

They strolled up Pitkerro Road till they reached the small park and the Stobsmuir Ponds, known locally as the Swannie Ponds due to the continual residence of a family of swans.

"Let's sit here," said Euan, "let the fresh air do its job."

THE PEPPER GIRLS

The air was cold but breathing deeply Annie began to relax and ease her mind about John when Euan spoke into the silence.

"That letter you got from Ireland at Mary Anne's christening, do you remember?"

Annie felt her blood run as cold as the air around her.

"You never did say what it was about and I've often wondered, was it bad news?"

A flock of thoughts flew through Annie's mind. Surely Euan couldn't have found any of John's letters to her, she had been too careful. Maybe Lexie had read that first letter and had only just told Euan, but she discounted that immediately. She searched for words to reassure him and herself.

"Letter?" she queried, "from Ireland."

"Yes, Annie, you must remember, you were quite upset at the time."

Annie pretended ignorance while Euan waited for an answer.

"Oh, **that** letter," she finally said. "It was nothing really, just the nuns from the poorhouse letting me know that Bella had made a good life for herself as a housemaid and that they were very proud of how she'd turned out."

Euan nodded. Annie was lying, he knew that and whatever it was she was hiding, he wasn't going to find out by badgering her.

"And do you still write to Bella?" he asked.

"You know I do," Annie countered, "in fact, I was hoping she might manage to come to Dundee for a visit sometime..." Her voice began to falter, she hated lying to her husband but the truth was too much to handle. Quickly, she changed the subject.

"We'd better be going home now, Ian will soon be back from school and he'll not be happy if he finds a locked door."

Euan sighed. His policeman nature had been well and truly aroused and instinct told him something was going on and he determined that he wouldn't rest till he found out what it was.

Ian rushed in just behind them, starving as usual and raided the cake tin before Annie could stop him.

"You'll spoil your appetite for your tea," she chided, "get on with your homework and learn some patience."

Tea turned out to be a rushed affair, as Ian had football practice and Lexie was meeting Charlie to go to the pictures and Annie found herself alone with Euan once more, keeping her fingers crossed that he'd say no more about any letters.

She babbled on about everything and nothing, never allowing Euan to get a word in edgeways. Ian bounced in around eight o'clock and promptly went to bed and when the clock struck ten Annie began yawning dramatically and indicated her intention to get some sleep as she was exhausted.

Euan became even more suspicious. What was going on with Annie!

"Night then," he said, "I'll just wait up a little longer till Lexie comes home."

Annie breathed a sigh of relief. Tomorrow it would all be forgotten and Euan would stop looking at her with those questioning eyes he usually kept for the wrongdoers at the jail.

But Euan had another reason for waiting up for Lexie. She knew something about that letter, he was sure and he was going to find out what it was.

Lexie duly arrived home at ten-thirty. "Still up, dad?" she called, popping her head round the parlour door.

Euan tapped out his pipe and beckoned Lexie to come in and sit down.

"I've been waiting up for you," he said, "there's something I want to ask you."

Lexie immediately felt for the ring through her jumper. Surely he didn't know about her secret engagement. She waited expectantly, holding her breath with guilt.

Euan cleared his throat. "Do you remember at Mary Anne's christening that your mother got a letter from Ireland that seemed to upset her?"

Lexie breathed a sigh of relief. "Yes," she responded cautiously.

"Did you ever find out what was in that letter?"

Lexie shook her head.

"She never said anything to me," she continued, "though I asked her more than once what it was about. I think maybe it was something to do with her friend Bella, but I don't know for sure."

Euan nodded. "That's what she told me too."

Lexie waited. "Was there anything else?" she asked, longing now to get to bed. She had work to go to tomorrow.

"And, what about now?" he asked, "do you think she's still upset about that letter?"

Lexie shrugged. "I've not noticed anything," she replied, "why are you asking?"

"No reason," Euan replied, "just curious."

"I'll say goodnight then."

"Yes Lexie, goodnight, sleep tight."

Maybe he was imagining things, after all he'd been working extra shifts since the turn of the year and he'd just got over tired.

He switched off the lamp and damped down the fire. Maybe tomorrow, he surmised, I'll forget all about it.

But next day and for many days after that, Euan didn't forget, in fact, he became more and more concerned.

Chapter 6

The call from Mr Mackay for Billy to come to his office, came a week after his visit to Billy Dawson.

"Come away in Billy," Mr Mackay beckoned, "I've some news for you." The Mill Manager shuffled some papers on his desk and checked his pocket watch. Billy stood very still and waited. His whole life felt like it was on hold, surely, his luck had turned and Billy Dawson had found work for him at Baxters.

"Yes, Mr Mackay," he finally voiced anxiously, "what's the news?"

"The news is, Billy," the manager intoned, trying to hide a smile that was threatening to break through his gruff exterior, "there's a full time job waiting for you at Baxters at their East Port Calender. Not as a spinner, I might add, but in the Batching House, starting Monday."

Relief washed over Billy. Full-time work at Baxters. Billy Dawson had been true to his word. Mr Mackay extended his hand. "You're a good worker Billy and Cox's loss will be Baxters gain."

Billy almost shook Mr Mackay's arm off.

The manager extracted his hand from the young man's grip.

"But there's also a little matter of accommodation," Mr Mackay continued, motioning Billy to calm down.

"Mr Dawson has arranged for you to lodge with a Mrs Kelly," he announced, taking a piece of paper from his waistcoat pocket and handing

26

it to Billy. "There's the address," he said, "and make sure you get there on Sunday for your seven o'clock start on Monday."

Billy gazed at the address, "4 Dens Brae."

"Will there be room for Nancy and the bairns?" he asked.

Mr Mackay sighed. "I'm afraid that's the rub, Billy," he told the young man, "it's just for you, till you get yourself settled in, then it's up to you to find a home for your family. I've agreed with the Mill Factor for Nancy to remain in her house for four more weeks, but then, she'll need to be out. Make room for other workers you know," he added, "so go tell that wife of yours the good news and I wish you both the best of luck."

Billy shook Mr Mackay's hand again. "Thanks," he said hoarsely," for everything." The manager nodded and waved Billy towards the door before he could see a tear forming in the old man's eyes. Life hadn't been easy for any of them of late, but for young men, like Billy and their families, the future seemed very grey indeed.

Billy couldn't contain himself as he threw open the door to the kitchen, causing Nancy to jump back in surprise.

"Billy?" she exclaimed, "what's the matter with you?"

Billy swept her into his arms. "Nothing's the matter," he grinned, "in fact, everything's fine, just fine." He released his grip on her and guided her to a kitchen chair. "Sit down," he urged, "I've got wonderful news."

Nancy waited, her face flushed and her heart racing. "Well?"

Billy pulled up a chair across the table from her and took hold of her hands.

"Your dad's only got me work at Baxters," he told her, "and it's full time in the Batching House, starting Monday." His grip tightened around Nancy's fingers. "Our worries are over," he smiled. "Mary Anne and wee Billy will never go hungry while their dad's around," he added proudly, "and as for you, my beautiful wife, you can get that new pair of boots you've been needing."

Nancy could hardly believe her ears. "Are you sure," she asked, "full-time and all?"

Billy nodded vigorously. "So, when do we move?" Nancy asked excitedly, looking around their sparsely furnished house, already planning how their belongings might fit into another room and kitchen.

Billy's joy diminished slightly, as we went on to explain to her that only he would be moving, but only till he found somewhere for them all to live. He didn't mention the four week time frame for this, but reassured Nancy it wouldn't be long at all till they were all together again. "And," he added brightly, "I'll come home every Saturday with a full pay packet to see that you and the bairns are fine."

He watched as the light went out of Nancy's eyes at this new piece of news. "I know it's going to be hard for a little while," he tried to assure her, "but we'll manage... won't we?"

But Nancy was already feeling the stirrings of panic forming in her stomach. With no husband coming home every night and no one to share her burdens with, she saw only fear for herself and her bairns.

"But, what if something goes wrong and I need you here," she asked, her voice trembling slightly, "wee Billy's not that strong yet and..."

Billy hushed her and came around the table to kneel at her side. "Nothing's going to happen to anyone," he told her, more firmly than he felt, "not you, nor any of the bairns." Nancy's eyes welled with fear. "It's only for a wee while," he said, "and Nan Duncan is next door to help if need be, just like she was when Billy was born."

Nancy felt defeated. She knew Billy had to take the work, but hadn't counted on him being away from her and their young ones for what could be weeks on end. She took a deep breath and met Billy's eyes with hers. "I know this has to be done," she agreed, "and I'll do the best I can to look after things here till we can be together again." Billy lifted her from the chair and pulled her towards him, careful to keep himself in control as her closeness brought heat to his body.

"I'll leave on Sunday night," he told her quietly, they've found me lodgings in a place called Dens Brae. "It's near the Calender and as soon as..."

Nancy held a finger to his lips. "Then, maybe we shouldn't waste any more time talking." She glanced over her shoulder to the double bed, sitting in the kitchen alcove. "The bairns are both asleep."

Billy felt all control go as she led him to the bed, dropping her shawl on the floor and slipping off her boots on the way. It had been a long time since they'd made love and it was almost too much for Billy to bear... but, he couldn't risk getting Nancy pregnant again, not after the doctor's warning about her health.

He pushed her gently onto the bed and kissed her forehead before turning away and heading towards the door through to the back room.

"Aren't you the lusty one," he chided Nancy lightly, "and me with a bag to pack." He disappeared into the darkness of the room, closing the door behind him.

His frustration almost drove him back into the kitchen again, but fear of the consequences kept his feet rooted to the spot. The move to Dens Brae might be a blessing in disguise, he told himself, willing the passion inside him to subside. His need for Nancy's love had become more urgent the more he saw of her and some time apart, he decided breathing deeply into the dimness, could only help to settle things down.

By the time he'd packed a few things in an old shopping bag, Nancy had steadied herself and was calm and cool when he returned to the kitchen. Billy tried to make light of his rejection of Nancy's advances, but only managed to make things worse.

"So, if you're going," she said icily, "there's the door." They both stared at the wooden structure, rather than look at one another.

"Right," Billy said, "I'll be off then." But there was no goodbye kiss or any indication that he would be missed.

Billy felt an anger tighten his muscles at Nancy's indifference. Didn't she understand anything about what he was going through? It wasn't his fault that he had to go to the other side of Dundee to get work, it wasn't his fault that he couldn't take her with him and it wasn't his fault that he couldn't love her like he wanted to.

He walked out and slammed the door on the silence. If that's the way she wanted it, he reasoned, so be it. She'd soon change her tune when the money started rolling in, he was sure.

But for Nancy, no amount of money could make up for the desolation she felt, not just at Billy's angry departure, but that he'd rejected her so totally, when all she'd wanted was to feel safe and loved. It was going to be a long and lonely week, with the prospect of many weeks like it to come. She bent over the sleeping form of her son, nestled in his crib and wondered at the peace of the sleeping infant. But for Nancy, there would be no peace, not until Billy came back and this time, she decided, he would love her like he used to, she'd make sure of that.

Chapter 7

After all the drama of Lexie's non-engagement had subsided, the whole family seemed to go back to domesticity with relief. Lexie and Charlie continued their courtship, safe in the knowledge that, when the time was right, they would reveal all to Annie and Euan who would immediately accept that their decision had been wrong and begin planning the wedding.

But for Annie, with one disaster averted, she now had to think about how she would manage to meet with her son without anyone knowing, especially not Euan.

But as she watched the letterbox every day for a letter from John telling her that he was now in Dundee, to start his student exchange visit, Euan was just as diligently watching her.

He just knew there was something disturbing his wife and he knew it had something to do with that letter from Ireland, but apart from searching through her things for any 'evidence', which his conscience wouldn't allow him to do, he had to content himself with biding his time and keeping his eyes peeled.

Then, on a cold morning in February, after Euan had left for the early shift, the letterbox rattled and Annie ran to the door. The letter she'd been waiting for and also dreading, had arrived.

Dear Annie

Well, here I am in Dundee and getting settled into my lodgings in Union Street. I start at the Infirmary in a week's time, so maybe, perhaps, we could arrange to meet before then. I'm longing to see you in person and can't wait to hear all about you and your Scottish family.

Let me know when and where and I'll be there.

Your son,

John

Annie reread the letter, just to make sure it was really happening. She would meet her son, at last, and somehow or other, she would do everything in her power to make him love her as she loved him.

She clasped the letter to her chest and with heart and mind racing, she penned him her reply.

Dearest John

There's a big church in the Nethergate, not far from your lodgings. It's always open and very quiet and I'll meet you there on Wednesday next at 11 o'clock.

Take care till then.

She didn't sign it, not knowing whether to put her name or call herself 'mother'. She folded the small note and would post it off to him on her way to visit Nancy in Lochee. She hadn't seen the new arrival and only had Josie's word for it that everything was fine. She would take something with her for the bairn and a sweet treat for Nancy.

Hurrying through her domestic duties, Annie finally donned her coat and hat and clutching the precious letter, left the house. "At last," she breathed. She would meet her son and all thoughts of being 'discovered' were put to the back of her mind. Nothing or no one mattered at that moment, not Euan, not Lexie and not Billy Dawson. Annie skipped down the stairs and, without hesitation, dropped the letter in the postbox.

It was a long tram journey to Lochee, but for Annie, time was now irrelevant. There was only one time that mattered, Wednesday at eleven o'clock.

Annie had to knock twice before Nancy came to the door, but her eyes were dark with strain and the bloom had, once more, gone from her cheeks.

"Why, Nancy!" Annie exclaimed, "what on earth's wrong?" Without waiting for an explanation Annie wrapped her arm around her niece and guided her into the small kitchen.

Mary Anne was crawling around on the floor, picking up whatever she found interesting and trying to eat it. Little Billy was grizzling in his crib.

Annie quickly took off her coat and hat and put the kettle on, while Nancy sat gazing into the middle distance, seemingly oblivious to the needs of her children.

"Here," she said softly to Nancy, "drink this." She wrapped Nancy's fingers round the cup of hot, sweet tea and waited. Something was very wrong. And, where was Billy?

The tea brought a faint flush of warmth to Nancy's cheeks, but her eyes were still bleak.

"Billy's gone," Nancy stated flatly.

Annie flinched. "Gone," she repeated, "gone where Nancy?"

"Gone to work," came the short response.

Annie's brows furrowed, not understanding her niece's reply. "But Nancy, that's nothing to be upset about, surely, isn't it good that Billy's working?"

"You don't understand," Nancy whispered, her eyes dropping to her hands, tightly curled in her lap.

"He doesn't love me anymore," she blurted out, "not anymore." Tears began to flow down her young face.

Annie became more confused and grasped Nancy by her shoulders. "You're not making any sense, Nancy," she said, the panic in her soul showing in her voice.

With much cajoling, Nancy eventually told her the whole story.

"And he just left, without saying goodbye?"

The distraught Nancy nodded.

"I don't know what I'll do without him," she wailed, "he'll never come back to me, not ever."

Annie could see she was getting nowhere and Mary Anne was getting dangerously close to swallowing something grey and hard she'd found under the table.

"C'mon," Annie announced briskly, "you're coming with me till we get this sorted. I'll get Mary Anne's coat and you get Billy sorted and Nancy, I'm here now, so everything will be alright." Annie said this with more assurance than she felt. Her first stop, after getting Nancy and the children safely to her home would be to seek out Billy Dawson and ask him what all this was about.

The journey back to Albert Street was uneventful, both women lost in their own thoughts about the future. Annie only knew that she had to get

Nancy out of that house, there was no telling how things would end up if she had left her there alone with the bairns.

"The next stop's ours," Annie said, holding wee Billy tightly as the tram trundled to a halt. Nancy took Mary Anne's hand and followed Annie off the tram and into Albert Street.

"We're not far from Dens Brae here, aren't we?" she asked Annie, looking back down Albert Street and brightening visibly at being nearer to where Billy was to be living.

"Let's just get you in," Annie countered, "there's been enough drama for one day." How like her mother Nancy was. The same emotional reactions to everything, the ability she had to have others sort out her problems for her and, of course, her mother's looks which caused some men to lose all reason.

Euan was just back from his shift at the Police Station and if he was shocked at the unexpected arrival of Nancy and her two bairns, he didn't show it.

"What's happened?" he whispered to Annie as Nancy took the children into the kitchen.

"It's a long story," Annie replied, "and I think I'm going to need Isabella Anderson's help with this one, if I'm not mistaken." She looked at Euan with practical eyes. "Can you go to the Salvation Army Hall and see if you can get a message to her, Nancy and the wee ones are going to need a roof over their heads for a while and we've no room for them here."

Euan nodded. At least they weren't going to have another argument with Lexie about sharing her room.

Euan pulled on his tunic. "I'll do my best," he said, much to Annie's relief. She could always rely on Euan, she realised, even when she didn't deserve his understanding. For a second she regretted posting the letter to her son, but it was too late now, the die was cast. But for the moment, there were hungry little mouths to feed.

True to his word, Euan returned later that day with Isabella in tow.

Annie hugged her sister-in-law and explained Nancy's plight.

"I don't really understand what it's all about," she told Isabella, "but I need to speak to Billy Dawson as soon as possible and get this sorted out."

Isabella agreed, but not before offering Nancy and her children lodgings with her and John at their home in Janefield Place. "They'll be fine with us till things get back to normal," she assured Annie, "and as I'll never be a

Grannie myself, it will be a rare treat for me to have two young ones around the place."

So it was decided. Annie had rescued Nancy again.

Chapter 8

Thanks to the abrupt departure from his home, Billy turned up at Mrs Kelly's door that Saturday night. He wasn't used to being in the east end of Dundee, having lived all his life in Lochee and didn't know where else to go. Going to Billy Dawson again for help wasn't an option.

The close Billy was looking for was located on the left hand side of Dens Brae, just past Todburn Lane. On the right hand side was the towering wall of Baxters Mill which ran all the way up to its junction with Victoria Road at the top. Billy craned his neck to look at the windows and dark closes that climbed steeply up the Brae, home to Baxters' workers and nodded to a cluster of women who stood at the end of Todburn Lane gossiping. As he bent to the climb, he could hear them muttering and nudging one another, but he kept his head down and quickly disappeared into Mrs Kelly's close.

There was a small piece of wood nailed to the front door, black with age and in sore need of painting. On it, Billy read the one word 'KELLY' and knocked.

The door was opened by a young girl, who eyed him from under the fall of fair hair drifting down the sides of her small face.

Her grey dress was to her knees and she had her hands hidden in the two front pockets. Billy checked the door again. "Is this the house of Mrs Kelly," he asked bending down to make sure she heard.

The girl nodded then quietly closed the door leaving Billy on the step. He knocked again.

This time the door was opened by a much older woman.

"Mrs Kelly?" Billy asked, removing his bonnet.

"Who wants to ken?"

"It's me, Billy Donnelly," Billy stated, "Mr Dawson said you have lodgings for me."

Mrs Kelly's eyes screwed up, trying to place the face.

"If that's so," she squinted, "whit are you dain' here on Setterday. It's Sunday yir expected."

Billy winced. "I know," he said, "I'm sorry, but I didn't have a choice."

The poor excuse brought back visions of Nancy and how distressed she had been when he'd walked out.

"I'll pay you a shilling for the extra night," he offered, "if you'd be so kind...?"

Mrs Kelly stood back and opened the door, indicating with a nod of her head that he should enter.

The inside of the house was as dark and depressing as the close outside, but it was clean and Mrs Kelly seemed reasonable enough. He looked around for the girl, but she was nowhere to be seen. Hiding, he surmised, and wondered at her relationship to his landlady.

He followed the crone through a narrow corridor to a short flight of wooden steps. She took an iron key from her apron and opened the door. Returning down the steps she handed the key to Billy.

"No smokin', drinkin' or prossies in there," she stated bluntly, indicating the room, "and the front door will be locked at ten o'clock git back any time efter that and you'll be locked oot."

Billy nodded. "Whatever you say, Mrs Kelly," he agreed, trying to affect a winning smile.

He watched her disappear back down the corridor and entered the tiny space. A single bed, a chair, a chest of drawers and a rag rug on the floor met his eyes. A whiff of paraffin came from a small lamp sitting on the top of the drawers. Billy took off the glass funnel and lit the wick. Weird black shadows danced over the wall as he returned the top and adjusted the flame.

"God help us," he murmured to himself, as he gingerly lay down on the iron framed bed. Only desperation stopped him from running out of this place and back to Nancy and the little ones. He closed his eyes, and felt the lashes wet with tears. He pulled the only blanket over his shoulders and willed himself to find sleep. Tomorrow could only be better, he determined and on Monday, he'd be out all day working. With this thought in mind, he cursed his religion, his lust for Nancy and his fear for the future.

The next day was no better, and after a solitary breakfast of porridge and tea, served by Mrs Kelly in her kitchen, he went out to get his bearings. Dens Brae and Todburn Lane were deserted at this hour on Sunday and he took his time to locate The East Port Calender in King Street. The huge arched stone entrance, where the horses and carts deposited the bales of jute from the warehouses were silent and foreboding. Tomorrow, they would be a hive of industry but on Sunday, nothing and no one worked. It was God's day and hell and damnation was the punishment to anyone who broke the Sabbath.

He wandered down King Street to St Andrews Street from where he could see ships masts in the distance. 'Must be the river and the docks down there' he decided heading in the direction. A pale sun was beginning to show from behind the clouds as he emerged into Dock Street, where the only other human around was an old man, sitting outside the Seaman's Mission on a wooden stool, puffing on a clay pipe.

"Mornin'," Billy said. The old man looked up and nodded, before returning to his pipe and his own thoughts.

Billy was getting more and more dispirited. He even thought of finding a chapel and going to Mass, after all, no one knew him here and he sorely needed to speak to someone. His life seemed such a mess and Nancy, what was happening to her now he was gone.

He walked along Dock Street to the Dundee West Station and turned up Union Street onto the Nethergate. Halfway up he saw the spire of a church and made his way towards it. It was indeed a church and its door was open. He ventured inside.

It was silent and peaceful and Billy wandered amongst the pews looking at images of Jesus at every stage of his suffering painted on heavy canvases that lined the walls. The pulpit and alter were ready and waiting for the congregation to begin arriving for the Sunday service, but for now, there was just Billy. Or so he thought.

"Can I help you?" said a deep voice. Billy swung around. The clergyman was smiling. "It's alright," he said, "this isn't my house it's God's and everyone is welcome here."

Billy relaxed. "I was just passing," he began nervously, "and, well, I just wanted somewhere to get my thoughts sorted out..." He laughed anxiously, "I'm a Roman Catholic, ex-communicated Roman Catholic," he added "and, well, I just needed..."

"Someone to talk to," the minister said, finishing the sentence for him. Billy relaxed and nodded.

For the next hour, Billy related all of the fears and distress he and Nancy had gone through since they'd met, including Joe Cassiday, Nancy's now dead stepfather and his obsession with her and how he and Nancy had fought before he'd left her to come to lodge in Dens Brae and work at Baxters.

The minister may have been a man of the cloth but he was foremost a man and his compassion for Billy and his plight moved him. He had come across this problem with the Catholic religion many times before and couldn't understand why they persisted in condoning the practice of turning lovemaking into a fearful thing for the woman and a frustrating thing for her husband. Surely, God wasn't that harsh.

The clergyman looked at his pocket watch. "Nearly time for the flock to arrive," he said standing up and offering Billy his hand.

"Come back anytime," he said, "the door's always open and I'm usually round or about. Things will sort out for you, I'm sure. Just have a little faith in that God of ours and let that lassie of yours know you love her."

It was with a lighter step that Billy returned to his lodgings. Tomorrow would be better and he would get word somehow to Nancy to say he was sorry and that he'd be back before she knew it. On his return to his lodgings, Mrs Kelly had made soup and offered him a bowlful for tuppence, including a doorstep of bread and butter. The smell of the broth made Billy realise how hungry he was and it was with a full stomach and easier heart he finally returned to his room. Tomorrow he would work hard and get word to Nancy that he'd be home soon. Yet again, the thought of Nancy awoke the desire in him, but finally he fell into a restless sleep.

Chapter 9

Now that Annie was taking control of things, Nancy began to feel that Billy would be persuaded to return to her. The last time she'd turned to Annie for help was when she'd became pregnant with Mary Anne and thanks to Annie's intervention, Billy had finally been made to see sense and had married her.

He had loved her then, she was sure of that, but what with the babies and the lack of money, he had somehow lost sight of that but to reject her, as he had done, was the final confirmation that Billy no longer loved her at all.

Annie and Isabella had gathered what they could of clothing for Nancy and the little ones to keep them warm and comfy, from the supply of clothing Isabella had brought with her and which had been donated to the Salvation Army for the needy.

"That should do it," said Isabella, folding the children's clothes into a shopping bag. "Now let's get them settled in at Janefield Place and tomorrow, you need to speak with Billy Dawson, find out what this is all about." Annie nodded and it would have to be at Billy and Josie's home, before Billy Donnelly started work on Monday.

Isabella and the little family left for Janefield Place and Euan offered to come with her to Billy and Josie's house. Annie readily agreed, meeting Billy Dawson was always a daunting experience for her and it seemed like she was always the one who needed his help.

There was a look of complete surprise on Josie Dawson's face when she opened the door to Annie and Euan. They never visited her home unless something was wrong and her mind raced up a hundred dead ends before admitting defeat.

She called over her shoulder into the gloom of the lobby. "Billy," she said, "it's Annie and Euan MacPherson come to visit." And to Annie and Euan she said, "come away in, we've just finished our Sunday meal, but I'll soon get the kettle on and make us some tea."

Annie and Euan followed her into the parlour where Billy was already standing, a look of confusion on his face.

"Well, this is a surprise," he told Euan, shaking his hand and offering him a seat. "And Annie," he continued taking her hand and guiding her next to Euan on the sofa, "how nice to see you."

Annie could feel Josie's eyes burning into the back of her head.

"I'll just make us all some tea," she said, moving towards the door, but Annie felt sure, she would be listening behind it.

"I'll get straight to the point," Annie began. "Nancy and the bairns are being looked after by Isabella Anderson for the time being, till Billy comes to his senses."

Billy looked more confused. "Comes to his senses about what?" he asked.

"Nancy tells me he's deserted her and the little ones, he doesn't love her anymore and it's all thanks to you!"

"Annie," Billy began, "it's not like that at all. Billy came to me asking for work and he starts at the East Port Calender on Monday and because he can't take the tram every day I've arranged for him to get lodgings with a Mrs Kelly during the week and go home to Nancy on Saturday with his wages."

Annie felt herself colour to the roots of her hair. Nancy had sent her off on a wild goose chase, just like her mother used to do and now she'd involved Isabella and Euan in the mess and all for what?

"So, he hasn't left her?" she asked apologetically.

Billy shook his head. "If she wants to see him, all she has to do is go to Mrs Kelly's door on Dens Brae."

Euan coughed theatrically. "Well, Billy, sorry to bother you but the way it was put to us, Billy had deserted her and the bairns without even a goodbye."

Josie entered with the tea things, a look of relief on her face.

For one horrible moment, she had felt her life with Billy slip away from her, till she heard the real reason for their visit.

Annie rose. "I'm sorry Josie, to have troubled you both, but we need to be getting on, so we'll not have time for the tea."

And with that, Annie, still red faced with embarrassment and Euan following behind her, made for the front door.

"I'll have a word with Billy on Monday," Billy Dawson called out to their backs. "Make sure everything's alright."

After they'd gone, Billy took the tea Josie offered him and allowed his breathing to ease. It was always the same, he thought he was over Annie Pepper, had been since Mary Anne's christening, but still, her unexpected arrival at his home had turned his stomach into a knot of desire again. And Josie saw it too.

Billy Donnelly turned up at the Calender at seven o'clock on Monday to be met by Billy Dawson. The two men shook hands.

"Did you find Mrs Kelly's alright?" Billy asked.

"I did," replied the young man, "and I think the lodging is just fine."

"And, what about Nancy and the bairns, how are they?"

This threw Billy. "They're also fine," he replied, wondering where this conversation was leading to.

"That's not what I've heard," Billy stated. "In fact, she's not at your home in Lochee, she's living with Isabella Anderson, saying you've deserted her and your children, left her without even a goodbye!"

Billy threw his head back in exasperation. "I haven't deserted her," he said, "nor the bairns. She was upset because she couldn't come with me and we had a bit of a row, that's all." He looked at Billy Dawson for understanding.

"Is that all it was?" Billy asked.

Billy hung his head remembering the rejection of Nancy's offer of lovemaking thanks to his concern for her health should she be with child again.

Billy could see there was more and pointed the lad in the direction of the Buckie, the small office above the loading bay used by the clerks.

Billy told him everything, about the premature birth of wee Billy, Nancy's fragile health, the doctor's warning and the fear that was his Catholic upbringing, eating him up every time he wanted to love Nancy, but couldn't.

Billy crossed his arms. Once again, he saw the young man torn between his love for his wife and his religion. "I thought you'd given all that up, Billy, the mass and confession and all when you and Nancy were wed?"

Billy shook his head. "I can't help what I feel," he murmured, "and it's the only way I know of to keep Nancy safe and alive."

"You're a young man Billy," he said gently, "with a young man's needs. How long do you think you can keep this from Nancy?"

Billy shrugged. "As long as I have to."

The Calender foreman came into the Buckie. "Ready to start," he said, nodding to Billy.

"Please, Mr Dawson," he said, "don't upset her further. Tell her I'm fine and I'll come and visit her soon."

The clatter of the hooves of a huge Clydesdale horse being backed into the loading bay ended all conversation. Billy needed to work off his frustration and his father in law needed to see his daughter.

The street lamps were being lit by the leeries when Billy decided he could probably sleep now and headed off in the direction of Mrs Kelly's lodging house. The work had been physically hard that day, but Billy was more than able for it. It kept his mind off Nancy and staying away from his lodgings till it was too late to do anything but sleep, seemed to be working. He only hoped that his father in law wouldn't stir up any more emotions in his wife till he was able to see her and maybe even try to explain himself.

There were three heads clustered around the table in Mrs Kelly's kitchen, a grey one, a dark brown one and a fair one, all filling their plates from a central iron pot of Stovies.

Mrs Kelly looked up as he entered. "You're late, Mr Donnelly," she told him, "but if you're quick there's still a good plateful left."

Billy pulled up a chair. His stomach had been in such a knot all day he'd managed to eat nothing, but now, with the thought of sleep just a room away, his appetite returned. He spooned the Stovies onto his plate, they smelled and looked rich and tasty and Billy lost no time in clearing his platter.

The women watched him, especially the one with dark brown curls, as he accepted a large mug of strong tea.

"I think yi've met mi granddaughter, Tilda," she said, indicating the fair one, "and this," she continued, "is her mither and my daughter, Gladys."

Billy nodded to the newcomer. "A pleasure to meet with you," he smiled, his eyes resting on her face which was smiling back at him.

"Gladys here works when she can," she explained, "but with a bairn to look efter, it's no' easy makin' ends meet."

"An' whit aboot yirsel'?" Gladys asked, leaning forward across the table and glancing from his eyes to his hands and back again. "In the Mill ma' says." Mrs Kelly settled herself at the fire and lit her clay pipe and Billy suddenly didn't feel tired at all.

"East Port Calender," he told her, "just started today."

Gladys seemed pleased to hear this. "So, what's a fine man like yirsel' doin' in lodgings," she queried a knowing gleam in her eyes.

Billy hesitated for only a split second before saying, "Not married Gladys," he lied, "free as a bird, so lodgings just suit me fine."

There was a moment of silence while Gladys tried to get the measure of the handsome Irishman in front of her. Pickings had been lean of late and to have a waged man living at her mother's lodging house and, available, seemed too good to be true.

"Tilda," she said to her daughter, "why don't you help grannie with the dishes, while me and Mr Donnelly get better acquainted through in the parlour." When her mother was eyeing up a 'prospect' Tilda knew better not to disobey and quietly bent to the task of clearing the table, while Gladys led Billy by the hand through to the cramped parlour.

She patted the sofa beside her. "Here," she said softly, "come and sit by me and tell me all your troubles, and we'll see what we can do to take them all away."

Billy shook his head. "No troubles," he said hoarsely, "just lonely."

Gladys was no fool. She'd met plenty of these young Irishmen before, always in heat but petrified of the priests and the confessional. "Is it a bit of love you're after," she queried grinning.

Billy nodded silently. "Then if you've the price of a quart of gin," she told him, "you can ha'e me."

Billy was so aroused, he couldn't have put a stop to things, even if he wanted to, not that he did. This wasn't being unfaithful, he told himself, Gladys was a prossie. Shakily, he rummaged in his pocket and produced a 2/- coin. Gladys slipped the coin under the doily on the small table beside them and unbuttoned her blouse.

The weeks of frustration coursed through Billy as he watched her remove her top and then her skirt, leaving only her underwear and boots.

"And now," she said huskily, "let's get you bare naked."

Chapter 10

Lexie was bored. It was Saturday morning and she was lying on her bed, gazing at the ring on the chain around her neck. She'd be seeing Charlie later that day, but it would just be the usual Saturday night, she knew, go to the pictures or for a walk or just sit in the parlour with Annie and Euan playing draughts or dominoes. Being secretly engaged wasn't half a much fun as she'd thought it would be, in fact, she was beginning to feel like an old married woman. Except, of course, there was none of 'that' going on and Charlie seemed to be quite happy to make do with the odd kiss and cuddle and wanted no more.

What was wrong with her, she chided herself, throwing back the covers and pushing her feet into her pink slippers. But she'd been thinking more and more about what it would be like when Charlie and she eventually 'did it' and this thought was making her feel 'funny' inside.

She flung off her nightgown and looked at herself in the Cheval mirror in her bedroom, twisting and turning to see herself from every angle. She knew she was pretty and that all the draughtsmen's eyes were secretly on her every time she walked through the Drawing Office at Baxters to go to her typewriter. She shook the thought from her head.

"Get yourself dressed Lexie Melville," she told herself sternly, but a part of her didn't want to get dressed and that was the part that she couldn't stop thinking about.

Annie was busy in the kitchen, as usual, trying to keep Ian above the 'starvation level' he always seemed to be at and Euan was cutting into his eggs and bacon when Lexie tripped into the room.

"You alright," Annie asked, "you're looking a bit flushed."

Lexie shrugged. "Fine," she said.

"Hope you're not coming down with anything," her mother continued, "there's a lot of flu about."

Lexie felt her cheeks burning, surely her mother couldn't see inside her head and know the thoughts she'd been having.

"I'm fine," she repeated firmly, "just bored," she added sitting down and trying to read the back of Euan's newspaper.

"Well, if it's bored you are," Annie said, "maybe you could get a few messages for me in King Street and pick up the meat order from Harry Duncan's."

"I s'pose."

Euan glanced at Lexie. "Manners," he intoned, "don't cost anything, even when you're bored."

Lexie turned her blue eyes on Euan. "Sorry."

The rustle of the newspaper being returned to Euan's face ended the conversation.

Annie put the toast in front of Lexie and poured her a cup of tea.

"Are you seeing Charlie later," she asked conversationally.

"I s'pose," Lexie said again, "we'll probably go for a walk or something..." Her words drifted off as the toast filled her mouth.

Annie shook her head. She knew her daughter of old, impetuous, emotional, always ready to leap in where angels feared to tread, but this was a side of her that was new.

Her thoughts turned to the meeting she was to have with her son, John, next Wednesday and she tried to imagine Lexie's reaction if they were ever introduced. Looking at Lexie now, bored and becalmed, Annie thought it just might be alright, but Lexie on one of her tangents was another matter altogether. She put the thought to the back of her mind and gave Lexie the list of shopping along with a purse with the money.

"The basket's in the hall," she instructed, "and when you come back we can go to Isabella's and see Nancy and the little ones if you like?"

Lexie shrugged again and picked up the money and list while popping the last of the toast into her mouth, before heading off to her room to get properly dressed.

There wasn't much choice of clothing, but the mood Lexie was in, she couldn't have cared less if she had to wear a jute sack, and flung on an old jumper and her work skirt.

"I'm off," she called to her mother closing the door and descending the steps into the close that led out to Albert Street. It was a busy Saturday and the shops were doing a roaring trade.

The bakers were particularly busy as bread and pies were bought for that night's tea and scones and pancakes were flying off the shelves.

Lexie wandered down Albert Street into Princes Street where she bought tea, butter and sugar at Liptons Grocers.

Mr McQueen, the Green Grocer in King Street, welcomed her with a wide smile. "Lexie," he said, "my, but you get bonnier by the day."

Lexie blushed. She'd known Mr McQueen since she was a wee girl and he used to smuggle an apple out for her under the nose of his wife.

"Mum wants carrots, turnip and leeks to make soup," she told him, "and some nice tomatoes."

Mr McQueen weighed and bagged the purchases before placing them in Lexie's basket. "Now," said Lexie, studying her list, "just the meat order from Harry Duncan's, then I'll get the tram home."

Harry Duncan was busy as usual wielding his filleting knife into what Lexie thought was a pig.

"Hello Mr Duncan," she said, "I'm in to pick up mum's meat order, if that's alright."

Harry Duncan nodded and wiped his hands on a blood-stained piece of muslin. "Just be a tick," he said and disappeared into the back shop. Lexie waited, her eyes ranging over the bloody produce.

"Is Harry in," asked a deep voice from the doorway. Lexie turned and her stomach did an involuntary somersault. There before her was a tall dark and yes, very handsome stranger. A black trimmed beard and moustache set off a row of smiling white teeth and dark brown eyes gazed out from under a sailor's black peaked cap. His coat was open and showed a thick navy blue polo knit jumper over black trousers and heavy boots planted firmly in the sawdust on the floor.

Lexie could barely breathe. What was wrong with her!

"I said," the stranger repeated grinning at Lexie's discomfort, "is Harry in."

Before Lexie could get her voice back, Harry Duncan came through from the back shop, bearing Annie's meat order.

Lexie pointed to the stranger. "I think this gentleman's looking for you," she managed to say, covering her discomfort by re-arranging the basket to accommodate the meat, before moving to the door.

But her way was blocked. He was very tall and muscular and Lexie was no match as she tried to go past him.

"Don't you know me, Lexie?" he asked, his voice sounding like dark treacle, warm and dangerous. He knew her name!

"Do you no' recognise mi wee butcher's laddie," Harry Duncan said, enjoying the drama that was unfolding before him.

Lexie looked confused as a strong arm took the basket from her.

"Here," he said, "Lexie Melville shouldn't be carrying heavy baskets like this," he said, "allow me," and with that he guided Lexie and her basket out of the butcher's shop and into the street.

She could hear Harry Duncan laughing.

"Don't you recognise me Lexie?"

Lexie thought she was going to faint as her knees weakened.

"No," she said.

He threw back his head and laughed. "It's me," he told her, "Robbie."

Lexie was transfixed. "Robbie," she echoed. "Robbie Robertson."

"I've been away at sea for quite a while," he told her, "Merchant Navy. Been round the world, but home on leave for a couple of weeks, till I sign on again for the next trip."

Lexie couldn't believe it, not only did he not look like the Robbie Robertson she knew from her past, but he had an effect on her that Charlie never had, not even when they first met.

"Can I carry your basket to the tram stop?" he asked. There was that voice again, washing over Lexie like a warm breeze. She nodded.

For the first time in a very long time, Lexie was lost for words.

"You're even more beautiful than I remember," he whispered as he bent to take the basket from her. Lexie suddenly became aware of how awful she looked, old jumper and skirt and she'd even forgotten to brush her hair properly, pinning it up with a couple of combs to keep it out of the way.

The tram rumbled to a stop and Robbie handed Lexie her basket.

"I'm home for two weeks," he said, "maybe we'll meet again."

He touched the rim of his cap and stepped back while Lexie boarded the tram. She sat down with a bump, overwhelmed by what had just happened to her and watching the broad back of Robbie Robertson as he crossed the road ahead of the tram. The last time Lexie saw him, he was a scruffy boy, but now, there was no doubt, Robbie Robertson was a man and a man of the world at that. She clutched the ring on the silver chain around her neck. She hated Robbie Robertson... didn't she?

Chapter 11

If Euan noticed anything different about Annie on the Wednesday morning, he didn't say anything. Just went about his usual ablutions and morning routine.

"Anything planned for the day," he vaguely asked Annie.

Annie jumped. "Planned," she repeated, guilt causing her voice to rise an octave. "No, no, nothing."

Euan raised his eyebrows. "I only asked," he said, now knowing something was in the wind.

He buttoned his tunic and bent to kiss her cheek. "I'll be back around two o'clock," he said, "maybe we could go for a walk if it's still nice by then."

Annie agreed. "That would be just fine," she said, "and maybe Nancy and the bairns would like to join us, get them out from under Isabella's feet for a wee while."

Mmmmmm, Euan thought, she didn't want to be alone with him. Yes, something was definitely going on.

"Right," he said, "well I'll be off. See you later."

Annie breathed a sigh of relief. She only had to get to the Nethergate for eleven o'clock and then the fates would decide how the meeting with her son John would go.

With Euan and her family now all gone for the day, Annie went to the wardrobe in her bedroom to find something suitable to wear for her first encounter with her son.

Her fingers trembled slightly as she shifted the items of clothing along the rail, frowning at the plainness of everything.

She finally settled for a cream blouse with a high collar and a brown wool skirt. It would have to do. She brushed her hair into a bun on top of her head and fixed it with a tortoise shell comb. Leaning forward towards the mirror, she examined her skin, running her fingers over the fine lines that had formed around her eyes and mouth and wishing she were twenty years younger.

The letter box rattled startling her negative thoughts, but it was only the postman delivering a bill and a letter for Euan. She tucked them into the space behind the tea caddy in the kitchen and looked at the clock.

It was only ten past nine. With nearly two hours to go before seeing him, Annie felt her nerves getting the better of her. What if he didn't like what he saw, what if he didn't want to meet her again, what if... Annie froze. What if he wanted to know the name of his father!

She wouldn't be able to tell him that Billy Dawson was his father, even if she wanted to. Billy himself didn't know he'd fathered a son, let alone that his son was in Scotland and about to meet her.

Annie clenched her fists and began to panic.

What can of worms had she opened? Why couldn't she have just left well alone and never written to John at all! But even as she chided herself, she knew that she couldn't have ignored the letter from Dr Adams telling her of her son's existence, let alone, not written to him as his mother.

By the time she was due to leave, she had calmed down, telling herself that she would meet him only this once, explain about Euan and her family and how she had their lives to consider, wish him well and leave it at that. It all sounded very reasonable in her head as she closed the door behind her, but in her heart there was only a deep longing to claim him as her own and love him forever.

The walk to the Nethergate helped settle her down and by the time she'd reached the church, she felt she could cope with whatever happened next. The heavy door stood open and Annie could see into the dimness of the interior. It was empty. Panic quickly enveloped her. He wasn't coming... he wasn't coming.

She moved slowly down the aisle, looking to left and right at the empty pews before finally sitting down in the front one and gazing at the wooden alter with the tall, brass candlesticks either side of it.

The bible lay open on the lectern surrounded by the silence of the morning and the image of the crucified Christ, sacrificed for her sins, hung before her.

An overwhelming guilt seized her. This was wrong, she told herself desperately, all wrong, meeting her illegitimate son in a church of all places, why hadn't she thought this through. Every fibre of her being wanted to run out of this place, put all this behind her, never see her son ever. But, her heart won again and she stayed, folding her hands in prayer and closing her eyes.

The first indication that she was no longer alone was the weight of a hand on her shoulder.

"Is everything alright?" the minister asked. "I'm the Reverend Mitchell, Alan Mitchell and you're quite welcome to stay here as long as you like, but if there's anything I can do...?"

Annie blinked her eyes open, feeling tears of despair forming on her lashes, but before she could answer, another voice reached her ears.

"It's alright," it said, "she's waiting for me."

The minister moved aside and there he was, her son, standing so tall and so handsome, just like his father had been all those years ago. She would have known him anywhere and a huge surge of love filled her soul.

"John?" she whispered. He nodded, smiling at the woman who'd given him birth.

"It's John," he said simply, "your son."

Forgetting all manners and everything else she'd learned about decorum, she flung herself into his arms, the tears now flowing unchecked down her face and her embrace was returned in full.

All the years of separation faded in that moment, all thoughts of meeting him only this once fled and Euan and Lexie and Ian were forgotten.

The minister realised this was no ordinary encounter.

"Would you care to continue your meeting in the Vestry," he asked gently, indicating a side door. John took his mother's hand and nodded.

For Annie and her son, time stood still and it was well after one o'clock before he'd told her all about his adoptive parents and his life in Ireland. Yes, he was going to be doctor and no, he didn't have a girlfriend and yes, he wanted to meet with his mother again and her family, if that was possible?

Annie skirted round that request and pushed it into the future. She wasn't ready to bring her son fully into her family life just yet, but maybe someday soon, she told him. He didn't ask about who his father might be and Annie felt relief that she didn't have to make that decision right now. She was just so happy to be united with John that nothing else mattered. But that was wishful thinking and she knew it. Euan, Lexie and Ian would have to be told, if she was to have any future with her son and as for Billy Dawson, that was something that held the most fear for her and something she didn't want to think about. Not today and not now, now that she had found her son at last.

They embraced goodbye and arranged to meet again in two weeks' time, but not at the church, this time they'd arranged to meet at The Howff, the old graveyard in Dundee and Annie would bring a picnic for them to eat amongst the gravestones. "Twelve o'clock then, mother," John said.

Annie felt a surge of pride. "Twelve it is," she confirmed, before watching him stride up the aisle and out of the church.

She waited a few minutes before searching out the Reverend Mitchell and thanking him for the use of his Vestry.

"It's none of my business," he said, "but has it been a while since you and your son were together?"

Annie smiled wistfully, "Too long," she said shaking his hand, "and now I must hurry, my husband will be home soon."

She boarded the next tram, her thoughts about what had just happened blinding her to the fact that she was being watched.

Constable O'Rourke from the Police Station where Euan was Sergeant was noting something down in his notebook. Euan would want to know about this.

Chapter 12

Billy went to see his daughter after the shift finished on Monday. Billy Donnelly could look after himself, but Nancy was a different matter and he wanted to hear from her own lips what had gone so wrong with the marriage that she had to be rescued from it and by Annie Pepper at that.

Isabella Anderson came to the door in answer to his knock. There was no love lost between the Salvation Army stalwart and Billy Dawson. He seemed to always be around when there was trouble and she blamed him as much for Mary's temptation to sin as she did her own husband's. If he'd been more of a man, she reasoned, Mary would never have left him, nor Nancy their baby daughter and ran off with her errant husband. But that was all water under the bridge now and John had returned to the matrimonial home, much chastened and grateful for Isabella's forgiveness.

"I believe Nancy's here with the children," he began, cap in hand!

It was more a statement than a question as she stepped back to allow him entry.

Mary Anne toddled towards him, looking so much like her mother and Nancy's mother, Mary, before her.

He swept her up in his arms. "And, how's grandpa's little girl then," he asked, ruffling Mary Anne's curls.

"Nancy's in the kitchen," Isabella told him, "she's just finished feeding wee Billy and putting him down, so quiet as you go," she instructed him.

He handed Mary Anne over to Isabella. "Do you mind?" he asked, "I need to speak with Nancy about Billy."

Isabella took the child. "Make sure he sees some sense Mr Dawson," she muttered, "deserting his wife and lovely family like that."

She bustled off into the parlour with Mary Anne waving over her shoulder to Billy. He knocked gently on the kitchen door and pushed it open. Nancy was at the table, folding some muslin nappies and her eyes lit up when she saw her father.

"There's news of Billy," she asked breathlessly.

Her father sat down holding up a hand to hush her. "He's fine Nancy," he told her, "I spoke with him this morning at the Calender and he's going to come to see you as soon as he can."

Nancy clapped her hands like a little girl. "I knew you'd make him love me again," she gushed, "now everything will be alright."

But the brittleness in Nancy's voice betrayed her misgivings and Billy was quick to notice it.

"Sit down, Nancy," he said, "we need to talk a little."

Billy could see the fear returning to her eyes. What was it that was troubling her so!

"Tell me about you and Billy," he asked, "since the new bairn... how have things been with you both?"

Nancy's eyes widened and her lip began to quiver. She cast her eyes down to her clenched fists.

"He's told you, hasn't he?" she murmured.

Billy moved his chair closer to her and tipped her head up.

"What has he told me, Nancy?" he asked.

"He's told you that he doesn't love me anymore..."

Her voice faded with the words.

"What makes you think that?"

Billy was her father, but she didn't care anymore who knew about her husband's rejection of her and his disappearance into the night, leaving her alone and wounded.

Damn the Catholic religion, Billy thought, making men choose obedience to the rules over love for their wives. Billy had to be made to understand, but he knew his fear of the priests was still firmly entrenched in his heart.

"Are you and the bairns alright with Isabella just now?"

Nancy nodded and her chin began to quiver again. "I just want Billy to love me again," she pleaded, "like he used to, before wee Billy was born." Billy stood up and turned to go.

"I'll see myself out," he said, "but I'll be back as soon as I can."

Billy had thought finding work for his son in law, albeit far from his home and Nancy, would solve everything, but it seemed to have uncovered a deep fear in him, which was going to be far more difficult to conquer. But conquer it he must for his daughter's sake.

The night was drawing in when Billy turned to walk up the steepness of Dens Brae to Mrs Kelly's lodging house.

A rush of memories of Charlie and Joe Cassiday crowded his thoughts. Nancy had been at the root of all that pain too and he fought to find something good in all of it. Joe dead for the love of her and Billy Donnelly, now living in fear that if he made her pregnant again, like his religion required, she could also die.

He pushed the thoughts aside and knocked on Mrs Kelly's door and waited.

He could hear a rush of activity, a chair scraping over the wooden floor and voices murmuring as the flicker of a lamp being lit glowed in the small window.

A pale face framed with brown curls peered round the corner of the door, her partly-dressed form being covered by a shawl, which she kept gathering tighter up to her neck. She squinted at Billy and called over her shoulder. "It's a man."

The door creaked open further and there was Billy Donnelly, his shirt hanging over his trousers and his head bent to the task of tightening his belt. He was barefoot.

It was obvious to Billy what he'd interrupted and had it not been for rendering Nancy a widow and the children orphans, he would have killed him on the spot.

Billy pushed a protesting Gladys behind him. "It's alright," he said, "I know who it is."

Gladys shrugged her shoulders and pulled the shawl over her bare arms. She'd been paid for her services and judging by the urgency of his lovemaking, she knew he'd be back for more and more.

"I'll wait for you at the end of Todburn Lane," Billy spat, "make yourself decent... if that's possible."

Billy Donnelly, rammed his feet into his boots and pulled on his jacket and hurried out after his father in law.

Billy lit a cigarette and exhaled the smoke into the cold night air.

So this was Billy's way of keeping his wife safe. No wonder Nancy had felt unwanted and unloved.

"Was that the first time?" he asked.

"You don't understand," Billy began, "she's a prossie, that's all, not a proper woman and she wouldn't take no for an answer..." His voice trailed off in the blaze of his father in law's eyes.

"A prossie, eh Billy, well, that makes it alright then."

Billy felt his muscles tense as he waited for a fist to slam into his gut, but it didn't come.

"So, that's alright then, is it?" Billy asked again, louder this time.

The young man locked his eyes on his boots and shook his head.

Billy Dawson understood better than anyone the temptations of the flesh and hadn't he gotten Nancy's mother Mary pregnant all that time ago in Ireland, but he had done the decent thing and married her, not gone and spent his time with prostitutes.

Billy inhaled the last of the tobacco. "Here's what you'll do," he told his son in law harshly, "you'll stop all this Catholic nonsense and do what the rest of us do, use a sheath and love your wife."

Billy began to protest, "But... "

Billy grasped him by the lapels of his coat. "You've given me nothing but grief since I first met you," he said through gritted teeth, "and if wasn't for the fact that Nancy loves you, I'd throw you to the wolves." He released his grip. "Now, get your things," he said, "you're coming with me."

Billy waited while young Billy disappeared into Mrs Kelly's house to gather together his few possessions and they were soon on their way back up to Morgan Street. "Where are we going?"

"You'll stay the night with me and Josie and tomorrow after your shift, me and you are going to Nancy's to ask her forgiveness and prove to her that you're a man and not a frightened boy. And, Billy," his father in law added, "make sure you wash yourself clean of the smell of that woman before you go anywhere near my daughter."

Chapter 13

The shock of seeing Robbie Robertson reverberated through Lexie for the whole of the tram journey and by the time she deposited the shopping on the kitchen table, she was decidedly hot and bothered.

"Are you sure you're alright, Lexie?" asked Annie, frowning at her daughter's high colour.

"I'm fine," she squeaked, "just fine." She looked at the clock, Charlie wouldn't be here for at least a couple of hours. "I'm just going over to Sarah's for a wee while," she said, hoping against hope that her old friend would be home, "be back before tea."

Annie shook her head. Since going steady with Charlie, Lexie had banished Sarah to the back seat, but it looked like they were still friends. Lexie knew she'd neglected Sarah since Charlie had come into her life, but she hoped she'd understand the urgency of her mission, once she told her about her encounter with Robbie Robertson.

It was Sarah herself who opened the door, a book in one hand and her spectacles pushed up to the top of her head. "Lexie," she cried, "what a surprise." She'd missed her friend but had reasoned that with Lexie, boys always took priority and anyway, she had something very, very interesting to tell her herself.

"Come in," she urged, leading her through to the bedroom. Lexie followed, shutting the door quietly behind her. She knew that Sarah's mother didn't really approve of her, but didn't care, as this news was so important, she just had to share it with her best friend no matter what.

The two girls settled down, Sarah sitting on the edge of her own bed and Lexie in the basket chair by the window.

"Well?" Sarah said, "you look pleased with yourself."

Lexie took a deep breath. Did her feelings show that much?

"Guess who I saw today?" she asked, leaning forward the clasping her hands tightly.

Sarah put on a thoughtful face.

"Don't know," she said, playing the game.

Lexie took another deep breath. "Robbie Robertson."

Sarah's look went from thoughtful to quizzical.

"So?"

"Sarah," began Lexie, a look of wonderment on her face, "he's not at all like you remember, he's been around the world with the Merchant Navy and he's home on leave and... Sarah, please don't tell Charlie I said this, but he's absolutely gorgeous."

Sarah started to speak... "But I thought..." but Lexie continued with her news.

"Not only that, he carried my basket to the tram stop and said he hoped to see me again while he was home and..."

Sarah held up her hands. "Wait a second," she squealed, "are we talking about the same Robbie Robertson who you hated and who you never wanted to see again as long as you lived."

Lexie nodded. "But that was when he was a boy. Now, he's a man and, Sarah, seeing him has left me with the strangest feelings of well... I don't know how to describe it. I just want to kiss him again and again." There she'd said it and she meant it.

"But what about Charlie?" Sarah asked, "aren't you and he going steady."

Lexie felt her bubble of euphoria burst. Of course, there was Charlie and she loved him, didn't she?

She looked at Sarah, the feelings she had experienced, beginning to soften and abate. "You're right," she said, "I don't know what come over me today, I think it was probably just the shock of seeing him again after all this time." The more her reasoning came in the calmer she became and with a big sigh, decided that she was just a silly girl and that Robbie Robertson was nothing more than a jolt from the past and best forgotten.

"Just remember," cautioned Sarah, "he'll only be here for two weeks, whereas Charlie will be here forever."

For some reason the thought of Charlie forever lowered her spirits even further.

"Well, I'd better be going," Lexie nodded glumly, "I said I'd be back for tea."

Sarah pulled at her sleeve, "But don't you want to hear my news?"

Lexie flinched. As usual she was so caught up with her own life that she forgot that Sarah had a life too. She sat back down again and waited.

"Well," Sarah began, warming to her turn in the limelight. "You know that I'm helping out at the Reference Library in Albert Square till my course starts at the University…" Lexie nodded, not another boring tale of missing books or the nuances of English grammar.

"Well, last week, a new young man turned up asking for directions to the medical section…"

"Yeeeees," Lexie urged, "so?"

"Soooooo," Sarah went on, "his name is John Adams and he's over here from Ireland on a student exchange for six months and, Lexie, he's the handsomest man you've ever seen." Lexie thought of Robbie Robertson and secretly begged to differ. She waited while her friend pulled her shoulders up to her ears and raised her arms above her head, "AND, he's only asked if he could perhaps take me out somewhere for a cup of tea next time he comes in, to thank me for my help and I hardly helped at all!" Sarah exclaimed, incredulously, her eyes gleaming. "Do you think it means he maybe likes me…?" The question went unanswered, as Lexie sat back, the significance of Sarah's announcement finally registering with her. A young man was attracted to Sarah? Not boring Sarah, with her books and her ambition to be an English teacher like her mum. Lexie could hardly believe her ears.

"Does your mum know about him?" she asked.

Sarah shook her head vigorously. "Oh no!" she countered rapidly, "it's nothing like that, we're just friends and anyway he's got his studying to do, so he won't have time for anything more than the odd cup of tea, I'm sure." She could feel herself blushing even as she said it.

"Why, Sarah Dawson," Lexie chided, "you're blushing."

Sarah's eyes were indeed sparkling at the thought of John Adams and Lexie's heart too was beating fast at the thought of Robbie Robertson. Both girls acknowledged their trust in each other's confidences, that this would go no further and Lexie returned home, calmer and willing herself to look forward to seeing Charlie while reminding herself continually that she hated Robbie Robertson.

Annie was putting the finishing touches to the table when Lexie came into the kitchen.

"Feeling better?" Annie asked, taking in her daughter's appearance which seemed to have returned to normal.

Lexie grimaced and quickly changed the subject.

"Guess what?"

Annie was spooning mashed potatoes into a bowl and trying to keep an eye on the cabbage bubbling on the stove at the same time.

"I'm not good at guessing," she told Lexie, her face hot from the steam rising from the mash. "Just tell me what it is?"

"Sarah Dawson," she said slowly, "has got a boyfriend."

Even Annie was surprised at this piece of news. She knew that Josie Dawson was vigilant when it came to any company Sarah kept and, unlike Lexie, had to account for her whereabouts at all times.

Annie smiled. "I don't believe you," she said, "her mother wouldn't allow it, not now Sarah's so near to starting her English degree."

Lexie began picking at the bread on the table. "Well," she continued, "that's because her mother doesn't know."

Annie started to drain the cabbage into a colander, beginning to wish that Lexie hadn't said anything to her, but curiosity got the better of her. "And where did Sarah meet this boy?" she asked.

"The Reference Library," Lexie said, glad that her mother was now more interested in Sarah's life than her own.

"The Reference Library," Annie echoed.

Lexie nodded vigorously, as she nibbled on the slice of bread.

"She's a volunteer there, helping out or something and this boy came in, well man really and now he's taking her out to tea to thank her for her help."

"And does this boy have a name?"

"John somebody," Lexie replied, now bored with the topic of Sarah and wishing to turn her thoughts again to the manly shape of Robbie Robertson.

Annie felt a twinge of fear form in her stomach. "And she didn't say what his last name was?" Annie tried to keep her words neutral and disinterested.

"Nope," said Lexie, now wishing her mother would stop asking all these questions. She already felt guilty about betraying Sarah's confidence for her own ends. "But, I think he's Irish or something."

Annie almost dropped the ladle she was holding, the colour draining from her face.

"Go tell Euan and Ian that tea's ready," she instructed Lexie, abruptly, hurrying to the sink and running the cold tap over her wrists.

If Lexie noticed a change in Annie's composure she didn't show it and went in search of Euan and her brother, calling, "Tea's ready," as she went.

"Calm down," Annie told herself, desperately, "it can't possibly be him. There must be hundreds of Johns in Dundee and at least half of them would be Irish." She splashed the cold water on her face and took a deep breath. No, no, no, she told herself, fate wouldn't be so unkind.

Euan and Ian came into the kitchen followed by Lexie and the whole family took their place at the table.

"Something smells good," said Euan, "as usual."

Silently, Annie began dishing out the beef stew and passing the plates to Lexie who dutifully put them in front of everyone.

"Help yourself to potatoes," she said over her shoulder, not ready yet to face her family, especially Euan.

There it was again, Euan thought, that faraway look, her distracted behaviour, her lame excuses for not joining in the conversation at the dinner table.

"Are you alright, Annie?" he asked.

Annie turned, pushing her hair back from her cheeks in an effort to cool them. She nodded, smiled and joined the others at the table. She began to play with the food on her plate, her thoughts racing.

What if, the John that Sarah was meeting was in fact her son, John Adams. Annie felt sick.

She pushed her chair back and stood up. Three pairs of eyes watched her, but none more closely than Euan.

"I... don't feel very well," she stammered, almost knocking over the chair in her haste to leave the room, "I'll just go for a lie down, I think."

Euan made to rise from the table. "No, please," she said as she passed him, "eat your dinner, I just need a rest."

Lexie and Ian shrugged their shoulders in unison and turned their attention back to their food. But Euan had lost his appetite.

He was sure now that something was far wrong with Annie and after the report he had had from Constable O'Rourke saying she had spent two hours in the Nethergate Church the previous Wednesday, he knew he had to find out what.

Chapter 14

By the time the shift had ended the following day, Billy had, once again, found a way to help his daughter. He'd spoken to one of his Masonic friends, who rented rooms and given his promise that he would guarantee the rent for a month, if he could find something quickly for the young family.

He was Nancy's father and would do anything for his daughter, but Billy Donnelly was a different matter. There was a weakness with the man, Billy feared, which had first shown up when Nancy fell pregnant to him, blaming his religion and fear of the priests for not being able to marry her. Billy had thought that he and Euan MacPherson had managed to set him straight on his responsibilities, but here he was again, using his religion this time as a reason for turning to a prostitute while Nancy waited at home alone feeling unloved.

But no more, Billy decided, this was the last time he was going to cover for Billy Donnelly, the man needed to grow up and quickly.

He was waiting at the entrance to the loading bay for his son in law and getting more agitated the longer he stood there. The image of Billy and Gladys Kelly was etched into his brain and the bastard would need more than God's help if Billy ever found out he'd repeated the performance.

Billy finally turned up, his hunched shoulders betraying his anxiety at meeting his father in law again.

"Have you got your wages?" Billy asked.

The young man nodded and showed Billy the unopened square brown envelope.

"Then, let's get going to Janefield Place and your wife and, Billy, don't even think about going back to Dens Brae, for any reason whatsoever, but especially not to see that woman."

Billy knew better than to say another word and together the two men walked up the steepness of the road to Janefield Place in silence.

When Nancy saw her husband, she immediately burst into tears and threw herself into his arms.

Her father watched the scene from the doorway, before imparting his news.

"There are two rooms waiting for you and your family," he told Billy, without a trace of a smile, "at 51 Victoria Road. The factor's known to me and he'll meet you there tomorrow with the key."

Billy looked incredulously at his father in law. He'd do all this for him and Nancy, then realised by the look on Billy's face that it was for Nancy only, that he was helping, and that he had no respect or liking for his son in law any more.

"Thanks," he said quietly to Billy, while Nancy ran into her father's arms with delight.

"I knew you'd sort everything out," she said, her eyes sparkling, "I just knew it."

Billy looked at his daughter, how like her mother she was, beautiful but eternally childlike, always in need of rescuing from something or someone. Could Billy Donnelly ever be man enough to be her protector? Billy thought not, but only time would tell and till then, he would watch and worry.

Isabella Anderson saw Billy to the door. "You're a good man Billy Dawson," she conceded reluctantly, seeing what had just passed between him and the troubled family.

Billy acknowledged the compliment. "They'll be out of your hair tomorrow," he told Isabella, "and let's hope that's the end of it."

But, it wasn't the end of it, not by a long chalk.

The following day, after a late night of talking and apologising all round, Billy and Nancy and their two bairns, began their new lives in the room and kitchen at 51 Victoria Road. The close leading to the tenement flats, was situated at the top of a steep slope and the kitchen looked towards William Lane below and onto King Street and Baxters where Billy now worked.

There was a railed walkway outside the row of doors where Nancy could park wee Billy in his pram and where the sun shone all afternoon in the summer.

Billy and Nancy spent all of Sunday carting their bits of furniture and pots and pans from Lochee to their new home. Mr MacKay at Cox's had arranged for one of the carter's to help with the flitting, again paid for by Billy Dawson and by the time everything was transferred to their new home, Billy and Nancy wanted to do no more than sleep.

The intended return to love making with Nancy, that her father had insisted upon, had yet to take place and Billy meant to delay this as long as possible. It wasn't just the fear of the Lord that hindered his actions this time, but the thought of his night with Gladys Kelly. It had been so carefree with her. No worries about pregnancies, or having to use the dreaded sheath and this, coupled with the thrill of being in dangerous waters, had greatly added to his enjoyment.

With Nancy, however, he felt it was always going to be a duty now, rather than a pleasure. But for Nancy, it was going to be for the love of her man.

The following day, she kissed her husband goodbye, with the promise of more when he came home from work and gathered her brood together. She loaded wee Billy into his pram with Mary Anne squashed in at his feet and set off to visit Annie and tell her all her good news.

She pushed the heavy pram up Victoria Road, then into Dura Street and finally to Annie's close in Albert Street.

Thankfully, Annie opened the door to her knock. "I'm fair whabbit," Nancy said smiling at her aunt, "so, if there's any tea going..." she added, angling the pram with its precious load into the lobby.

Annie forced a smile. She loved Nancy dearly, but the last thing she needed right now was to have her company. She was still reverberating from the news that Sarah Dawson had met a young man whose name just happened to be John and who was Irish and who could be, in Annie's guilty mind, John Adams her illegitimate son, unknowingly fathered by Billy Dawson.

She gathered herself together and picked up Mary Anne, carrying her tightly, like a life jacket, into the kitchen. At first Nancy didn't notice the distracted air around Annie, as she told her all about her new home with her now 'misunderstood' husband and how Billy Dawson had arranged everything and how wonderful a father he was.

Annie allowed all of this to go over her head, except the bit about Billy Dawson being a wonderful father. If only she knew the truth, would she still think him so wonderful?

Phased by Annie's lack of response to her good news, Nancy slowly realised something was amiss.

She put down her teacup and laid the now sleeping Billy back into his pram. "Is everything alright Auntie Annie," she asked, a note of concern now in her voice. Annie's eyes were bleak.

"Not really," she replied, "but I'm sure everything will be fine, given time."

Nancy frowned. What did that mean!

"Are you ill?" Nancy continued, trying again to understand Annie's answer and getting more worried at her lack of information.

"Oh, no, nothing like that," she said, "just a bit low, that's all."

How she wished she could unburden herself to her niece. Tell her all about her son and his birth in the poorhouse in Belfast and how he was now in Dundee and wanting to be part of Annie's family and life. And his father, Annie tensed at the thought. He would want to know about his father, Billy Dawson. It was all too much for Annie and tears began to course, unchecked, down her face.

Nancy was really concerned now, her aunt had always been the strong, capable one, coping with everyone's problems and looking after them all, but now...

"I'm sorry," Annie whispered as the tears abated. "I'm just being a silly old woman. Pay no attention to me."

She dabbed her eyes with her apron. She had to control herself, just for a few months, then John would be back in Ireland and things could return to normal. Till then, she had to carry on as if nothing was amiss and remember the consequences of anyone finding out, especially Euan and Billy Dawson.

The tears had eased the tension in her system and it was with the stoicism of years of coping with life that she assured Nancy that all was well and they would say no more about it.

But Nancy wasn't so reassured. Did Euan know how strangely Annie was behaving? She vowed to speak to him soon and find out what was wrong with her Auntie Annie.

Chapter 15

Try as she might, Lexie couldn't stop thinking about Robbie Robertson. She spent more and more time in her room, reliving the brief encounter at Harry Duncan's butcher shop and wondering how she could have ever hated the man.

Their puppy love, when she was still a schoolgirl, had resulted in Robbie and Lexie getting secretly engaged, but it was Robbie forcing his attentions on her that had scared her into putting an end to their romance. Then Euan's stern warning to the young lad that he should stay away from Lexie... or else, had been the end of it. But, Lexie always remembered what Robbie Robertson had done to her and it had coloured her unexciting courtship with Charlie, until recently, when she'd began to experience deep sexual urges. And now, Robbie Robertson was back and was as handsome and dangerous looking as the stars she had seen at the Picture Show, these urges were becoming almost unbearable.

Every day, when she finished her work at Baxters, she would cross over to the butcher's shop on her way to the tram stop, hoping that Robbie would somehow turn up again, but he didn't and Lexie had to content herself with her relationship with Charlie, which was becoming more and more irksome.

It was nearly a week since her encounter with Robbie and she'd almost given up hope of ever seeing him again. She'd even stopped crossing the road to pass by the butcher's when she heard that voice again, calling her name as she stepped from Baxter's doorway into King Street.

She swung around and there he was, looking even more handsome than the last time and her heart stood still.

"Remember me?" Robbie said his eyes taking in every inch of her.

Lexie found her voice. "Maybe," she said.

Robbie grinned. "And here's me thinking I was unforgettable, like you."

Lexie could feel herself blush to the roots of her hair. Did he really think she was unforgettable?

Robbie took her arm and linked it through his, his fingers strong grip relaying their urgency. "I'll walk you to the tram stop," he told her, adding, "only if I may."

Lexie was transfixed and all thoughts of Charlie Mathieson were swept from her mind. There was only one man in her world at that moment and that was Robbie.

No words were spoken as the couple walked arm in arm to the tram stop, but their bodies were speaking volumes.

"I think we need to meet," Robbie said, his eyes never leaving her face, "and soon."

Lexie nodded and he squeezed her hand in his.

"Tomorrow night at seven," he whispered, "at the park gates, just like in the old days." Lexie felt herself start to tremble, remembering what had happened then, but this time, she felt more than willing to feel Robbie's arms around her and his body taking hers.

"Seven it is," she echoed as the tram trundled to a stop in front of her. Robbie helped her board and stepped back, his eyes watching her every move. He had no doubt about the effect he had on Lexie and smiled to himself at the thought of her lying to that boyfriend of hers, Charlie Mathieson about where she was going on a Saturday night and why she couldn't possibly be with him.

"Gotcha, Lexie Melville," he said aloud, "now let's see how you feel when I reject you."

Lexie was in a blind panic by the time she reached home. She had to get word to Charlie that he couldn't come over on Saturday as she was ill, no, not ill, he'd be concerned and come over anyway, that she had to comfort a sick friend. Her eyes lit up, yes that was it, she had to spend Saturday with Sarah, who had a bad cold and needed her company. There was no way in this world she wasn't going to meet Robbie.

She had to see Sarah, get her help. She'd understand the urgency, how could she not, now that she had feelings for the man at the library.

For the second time in a week, Lexie turned up at Sarah's door, looking even more flushed and bothered than before.

She hurried past Sarah and flopped down onto one of the beds in the bedroom Sarah shared with her two sisters.

"What on earth is it?" Sarah squealed, "you're behaving like a mad woman!"

Lexie, her eyes glistening and bright with emotion explained her predicament.

"So, I have to meet him Sarah, I just have to."

This wasn't good. Sarah had seen Lexie in many different moods, over the years, but this one was different. She was almost out of control.

"Alright," Sarah said, "alright. I'll drop a note in to Charlie tomorrow on my way to the library and hope that he doesn't ask too many questions."

Lexie grasped her friend's hands. "Oh, thank you Sarah," she breathed, "I'll never forget you for this."

"Are you sure you're doing the right thing?" Sarah asked. "After all, you and Charlie seemed so happy..." but Lexie wasn't listening, in her fevered mind, she was already in the arms of Robbie Robertson and didn't care about anything else, especially not Charlie.

Lexie made her way home from Sarah's breathing in the cold air in an attempt to bring her heartbeat down and steady her breathing. Her mother mustn't see her like this and start asking questions again. She just had to hold it together till tomorrow night at seven o'clock, when she would meet Robbie Robertson and whatever he asked of her, she would surely do.

She thought she'd loved Charlie, but what she felt for him was nothing compared to the desire she was feeling at the mere thought of Robbie Robertson.

At a quarter to the hour of seven, Lexie made her excuses to Euan and her mother, saying that she'd probably be late as Sarah would keep her talking about that boyfriend of hers. Annie felt the palms of her hands begin to sweat as they held her knitting needles.

"Don't be too late," Euan said, "church tomorrow."

"I won't," said Lexie, moving towards the door. Just another few steps and she'd be out of there and on her way to her tryst with Robbie.

Her heart was singing. How could she ever have let him go. How childish she'd been, she saw that now, but no more, now she was a fully grown woman and ready for the love of a strong man. She pictured Robbie in her mind's eye again and no one was stronger than him.

The lamps were lit all along Arbroath Road as she neared the park gates. They were locked but it didn't matter, Robbie would find another way in. She wrapped her arms around herself, trying to keep warm in her skimpy coat and ankle boots. She could hear the chimes of a nearby church clock. Seven o'clock. He'd be here any minute. She looked around, it was quite dark now and there weren't many people around, save for a dog walker who passed her without comment.

The cold was seeping through the soles of her boots now and her ankles were beginning to feel numb. The church clock chimed the quarter hour then the half hour, but there was still no sign of Robbie. Lexie began to worry. Something must have happened to him, he must have had an accident she told herself as she paced up and down in front of the gates. But, by the time the clock struck eight, Lexie felt a deep foreboding in her soul as she realised the truth. Robbie Robertson wasn't coming to meet her at all, not now not ever.

It was as though she had been blind, but now she saw, this was his revenge on her rejection of him and nothing more than that.

"Looks like he's no' comin' lassie," said the kindly voice of the dog walker, now on his way back home with his four legged companion.

Lexie could have wept. "Looks like it," she said through tight lips, as she turned to go home. From the darkness of a nearby close, Robbie Robertson watched the scene with a smile. His ego restored.

"You're home early," Euan said, as Lexie came into the parlour where he and Annie were listening to the wireless.

"Sarah's feeling better," she told them blankly, "but I think I've got her cold, so I'll just have an early night." She lay down on her bed, pulling the eiderdown up under her chin and spent the rest of the night gazing into the dimness of her room and wondering where she would go from here. She knew now that she didn't really love Charlie and it would be cruel to lead him on any further. And, as for Robbie Robertson, no matter how badly he had treated her, she still longed for his touch. Lexie was growing up fast.

Chapter 16

The day of Annie's next meeting with her son, in the quietness of the gravestones at the Howff Cemetery, dawned cold and clear. She had tried to put the thought of Sarah and her son out of her head and determined that she wouldn't mention it to John. Confirmation of the two of them getting to know one another was something she wasn't ready to face.

She packed a small picnic for the both of them in her shopping basket and set off feeling a mixture of happiness and fear. Euan was getting more and more inquisitive and seemed to always be watching her, especially when she came home from shopping or visiting Isabella or just from being out for a walk.

Lexie, on the other hand, seemed totally disinterested in everything. She still went to her work at Baxters and still saw Charlie at the weekends, but something seemed to be missing. Annie had mentioned it to Charlie, wondering if he knew if anything was troubling her, but he'd just shrugged and continued coming round as normal.

A month had now passed since John's arrival in Dundee and Annie was beginning to feel that no hand of fate was going to strike her, nor a bolt from the heavens turn her into a pillar of salt, so was gently allowing herself to perhaps ease up on the guilt trip she was on and just enjoy the company of her wonderful son.

She turned the corner into Ward Road but to her horror, bumped into Constable O'Rourke. What was he doing here she thought, immediately panicking, wasn't his beat over towards Lochee!

"Constable O'Rourke," she heard herself say, "a little out of you way aren't you?"

"Just covering the beat of one of the young bobbies, off sickly these last two days."

Annie looked past the policeman's shoulder. She could see John approaching the Howff gates and hoped against hope that he wouldn't spot her and call out her name.

"Something wrong," asked O'Rourke, wondering why Mrs MacPherson was suddenly trying to disappear into herself.

"No, No," Annie said rapidly, "just in a bit of a hurry."

She sneaked another look over the constable's shoulder and saw John enter the cemetery, without looking her way.

With a sigh of relief, she straightened up and smiled her best smile. "Well, I'll be on my way then," she said briskly, turning around and walking back the way she had come and away from the cemetery gates.

The Constable shook his head as he watched her turn down Reform Street and disappear from view. "Where was she going now?"

Sergeant MacPherson was right, he surmised, something about his missus was definitely not making sense.

Annie skirted around the narrow streets, off Reform Street, till she was once again at the Howff gates. She scanned the road breathing deeply. Constable O'Rourke was nowhere to be seen, but she could see John waiting for her and entered the gates into the quietness of the graveyard.

His eyes lit up when he saw her. "I thought you'd forgotten you were coming," he said, taking her hand and guiding her to one of the low flat gravestones near the back of the cemetery. "Is this alright?" he asked.

"Perfect," said Annie, beginning to unpack the food. They were out of sight of the main road. No one would see them here.

Once again, the joy of being with her son blinkered her to all else and it wasn't until he began telling her that he'd met a really wonderful girl last week, that Annie came back to reality with a bump.

Cautiously, she asked, "And where did you meet this wonderful girl?"

But even before he told her, she knew. "At the Reference Library," he said, "her name's Sarah."

A strange calmness came over Annie. Just when she thought that fate had left her alone, there it was, catching out the unwary in her.

"But you're not serious about her, surely," she said quietly, "after all you'll be going back to Ireland in a few months' time."

John laughed. "Of course not," he told her, "we're just friends that's all, but she's a bit special," he added, a wistful look coming into his eyes. It was then that Annie knew. John was falling for his half-sister and she had to put a stop to it, somehow.

A chill came into the air and rain clouds began to gather as mother and son stood to go their separate ways.

"It's going to be a while before I can see you again," John told her, apologetically, "the hospital is really busy and what with the studying an' all…" but Annie knew the real reason.

She nodded. "That's alright John," she said, "let's arrange to meet here again in a month's time say, which should give you a chance to get used to your duties at the hospital."

John was quick to agree. He loved seeing his mother, but he had another female to consider now who he couldn't wait to see again. They'd arranged to meet for tea and scones at the little cafe near the library and he hoped that Sarah wanted to see him as much as he wanted to see her.

But it was with a heavy heart that Annie turned to home. If John continued to see Sarah, it would only be a matter of time before Josie found out about it and then Billy Dawson would be told and then the truth about John's birth would have to be revealed, bringing heartbreak to the two of them and pain for everyone else. Annie stopped in her tracks. She slowly realised, that if anyone could put a stop to Sarah's budding romance it was Josie! She lived with the fear that Sarah would meet someone and turn away from her studies and her mother's plan for her to become an English teacher like herself. Annie could feel her spirits rise.

She would see Josie Dawson at the first opportunity, thanking God that Lexie had told her Sarah's secret.

With her mind fixed on a solution, Annie hurried towards home. On the way, she stopped in at Harry Duncan's butcher shop. She'd buy some lamb chops, she decided, especially for Lexie, who she felt needed cheering up although she still didn't know what was wrong with her daughter.

Harry was busy talking to a tall bearded man when Annie entered his shop.

"Be with you in a mo', Mrs Melville," he said, shaking the man's hand and wishing him 'cheerio.'

The man turned to go and looked at Annie, a smile flitting across his lips.

"Mrs Melville," he said cordially, "and how's that daughter of yours, Lexie isn't it?"

Annie stepped back, a quizzical look on her face.

"And who's asking?"

"You're daughter knows me," he said enigmatically, "she'll tell you who I am." And with that, Robbie Robertson left the shop, never looking back.

Annie eyed Harry Duncan in confusion. "What was all that about?" she said. Harry grinned.

"Did you no' ken meh auld butcher lad?" Annie frowned and shrugged her shoulders.

"Robbie Robertson," announced Harry proudly.

"He's turned oot to be a fine seaman in the Merchant Navy tae."

Annie was shaken rigid at the news of the return of Robbie Robertson and what was his reference to Lexie all about?

Surely not,... Annie thought, was this the reason for Lexie's sudden disinterest in everything? Robbie Robertson!

Chapter 17

Billy Donnelly slowly began to 'paper over the cracks' in his marriage but spent more and more time in the Thrums Bar than at home. He still gave his attention to the bairns, but it was more a reason for not giving his time to Nancy rather than his fatherly duties.

If Nancy noticed, she didn't say anything, just glad that Billy was back with her. True, the marital bed was seldom used for its true purpose, as Billy continually told her he hated using the deadening sheath and implying that it was somehow her fault that he had to do so.

Can't have you bringing another bairn into the world, he'd said and as it was something that Nancy didn't want either, she accepted the excuse for his reluctance to make love to her. She'd heard some of the other young women saying the same thing. It was just the way things were and you just got on with minding your bairns and having your man's tea on the table when he came home from the mill.

And domestic life would have probably continued in this fashion but for Billy's recurring thoughts about Gladys Kelly. He would relive their night of lust by closing his eyes and feigning sleep, while Nancy sat opposite him and knitted woollen cardigans for wee Billy and cosy pixies for Mary Anne.

She would often have to shake him awake to tell him it was time for bed, but this seemed to irritate him, so she took to going to bed most nights alone.

It was one Friday night a week or so later when fate tapped Billy on the shoulder. The Thrums Bar was packed with mill workers spending their wages on whisky and beer, the air thick with cigarette and pipe smoke and Billy Donnelly was in the midst of it. He was downing beer and not wishing to go home to Nancy, when he saw her. Gladys Kelly was in the Snug Bar buying bottles of beer, probably for her mother Billy decided, and looking as tempting as ever.

He quickly finished the last of his beer and left the pub, turning into the darkness of the nearby close, where he waited for Gladys to pass by.

It wasn't long before he heard her approaching. With a suddenness that startled her, Billy stepped out of the darkness and stopped her progress up King Street, almost making her drop one of the bottles of beer.

Billy said nothing, just stared at her and saw the smile of recognition cross her face and with it the pleasure of the memory of their last encounter.

Gladys leaned against the close entrance, handing Billy the bottles of beer. "Going my way?" she asked huskily.

Billy nodded. There was no chance he wasn't 'going her way.'

This is what he'd been dreaming of for weeks now.

They walked up King Street and turned into Dens Brae.

"Mind the way, do you?" she asked, her eyes travelling from his mouth to the level of his obvious excitement. She leant forward into the climb up the steepness of the brae, breathing heavily with the exertion.

Her mother was seated beside the coal fire, smoking a clay pipe and waiting for the black iron kettle to boil. There was no sign of the granddaughter and if the crone was surprised at seeing Billy, she didn't show it.

"That meh drink?" she asked, bluntly, pointing to the bottles Billy was carrying.

He handed them over to her and stepped back into the shadows of the kitchen.

Gladys nodded to the door which led to Billy's room.

"We'll no' be bothered in there," she whispered, "and ma'll soon be snorin'."

Billy felt a fleeting whisper of fear as he remembered his promise to Billy Dawson, but safe in the knowledge that no one would tell him anything, certainly not Gladys, he pushed it aside and followed her up the wooden steps and into the room.

Gladys lit the paraffin lamp and held out her hand.

"It's half a crown this time," she said, "seein' it's pay day."

Billy reached into his trouser pocket and extracted the money from his wages, handing it over to Gladys, his excitement building. Now he would get what he paid for, and more. Gladys was insatiable.

It had gone midnight before Billy crept out of the house in Dens Brae and completed the climb upwards to Victoria Road and his home with Nancy.

She'd be asleep by now, he was sure of that, but the thrill of Gladys astride him in the cramped bed would stay with him till daybreak. There would be no rest for him that night.

But Nancy wasn't asleep and rolled over to face her husband, her arm falling across his chest, but she was rewarded with the sight of his back as he turned away from her. Nancy sighed and wrinkled her nose. What was that smell? She must ask Billy about it in the morning, as she too turned her back to him and went to sleep.

It was gone six on Saturday morning when Nancy woke.

"Billy," she whispered, "you need to get up for work."

Billy grunted, his eyes feeling gritty and heavy.

Nancy got out of bed and pulled on her shawl. The room was cold and she tried to coax some life into yesterday's embers without success. She filled the kettle and set the porridge going, Billy slept on.

"Billy," she hissed, fearful of waking the little ones, "wake up, you've your work to go to."

Finally, Billy opened his eyes and faced the reality of the morning. He'd spent the night in heaven but now he was back in hell.

He pushed the covers aside and a strong smell of sweat and fish hit him. It almost turned his stomach and then he remembered last night. Billy Dawson had commented on a smell the last time he'd been with Gladys but he'd been too scared to notice it then, but now…

He cast a glance at Nancy and poured some hot water from the kettle into the enamel basin and soaped himself down with the facecloth, while Nancy stirred the porridge and pretended not to notice anything amiss.

But it was as he began to eat his breakfast that she spoke.

"You were late last night," she said, amiably enough, trying to conceal the worry in her heart.

"Aye," Billy responded not looking at her, "had a drink with some of the lads from the Calender and lost track o'time. Sorry."

"You must ha'e been drinking in an auld fish shop," Nancy added, "the smell that was on you."

Billy almost dropped the spoon.

"Smell?" he asked, feigning ignorance, "never noticed anythin'."

But Nancy persisted. "But it was awful Billy, like rotten fish or a manky auld cloth."

Billy pulled a face and slammed down the spoon. "Look what you've done now," he shouted, "put me right aff the porridge." He stood up and pulled on his jacket, muttering to himself as he went out the kitchen, slamming the door behind him.

The wailing of wee Billy prevented Nancy from dissolving into tears and she hurried through to the room to fetch her crying infant. Mary Anne had also woken up with all the shouting and clung to Nancy's skirt as she transported her offspring into the kitchen.

Billy was just tired, that was all, she told herself and probably still drunk from the night before. She chided herself for being so silly as to mention the smell before Billy even had a chance to waken up, but it still seemed to be lingering on the bedsheets. She'd take them all down to the wash house later and get rid of the smell, whatever it was, and never mention it again.

The weather seemed set fair for drying and Nancy piled the sheets into wee Billy's pram and piled the bairns on top of them. It was a long walk down to the public wash house in Constable Street but at least it was downhill, the walk back would be uphill all the way.

The wash house was busy with women from the mills going about their Saturday chores. Steam was everywhere and the noise of the women's banter coupled with the racket of the sinks and metal drying cabinets filled Nancy's ears.

She found an empty sink and having parked wee Billy back into his pram with Mary Anne to keep an eye on him, she set about filling the sink with cold water to loosen the fishy smell.

The young woman at the sink next to her gave her a knowing glance. "Dinna of'en see the likes o' you in a place like this," she said, "was there no' much business last night, hen, or maybe you're gettin' ready for better pickins' the nicht?"

Nancy frowned. "Whit do you mean by that?" she asked as she plunged her hands into the cold water.

The woman shook her head and smiled. "Well if you dinna ken the smell o' your fanny an' randy men on yir sheets, business must be slow."

Nancy felt herself wobble. She wasn't a prossie, she was a married woman with a loving husband...

The realisation hit Nancy like a sledgehammer. That was why Billy was late home, he'd been with a... Nancy could hardly bear to think the word never mind say it.

Leaving the sheets in the sink, she practically ran from the wash house. There was only one place she could go and that was Annie's.

Blinded by tears she pushed the pram with the bairns crushed in together up Princes Street and into Albert Street.

"Please be in," she repeated to herself as she turned into the close leading to Annie's door, but it was Euan who opened the door to her.

"She's over at Josie Dawson's," he said, "but she won't be long if you'd like to wait."

He could see Nancy was upset. This didn't bode well for Annie's return, so he did what he could to settle her and the bairns down as quickly as he could.

Euan filled the kettle. What was going on with all these women, he wondered, anxiously, first there was Annie, looking distracted and distant a lot of the time, Lexie brooding about something or someone and now Nancy, looking quite distressed.

He made a pot of tea for Nancy and gave Mary Anne some milk and one of Annie's shortbread biscuits and was just filling himself out a much needed cup of tea when Annie came in.

As soon as she saw her niece, she knew something was wrong again and felt certain it would concern Billy Donnelly.

But even Annie didn't expect the story Nancy told her.

"There's more trouble with Billy," she said to Euan, when Nancy had gone for a lie down with Mary Anne and wee Billy was settled in his pram.

Euan shook his head. "I'd hoped he'd grown up since Billy Dawson had a strong word with him, and he'd married Nancy, but it doesn't look like it."

Annie sank into a chair. She was having to cope with so much intrigue and lies of her own that she was almost drowning and now this.

She felt Euan's arm around her. "You know I'm always here," he said, gently, "and if you want me to have a word with young Billy about all this..." Annie could have cried. Here was this man who loved her and cared for her and there she was deceiving him about Billy Dawson and her past and worst of all, her bastard son.

She nodded. "Yes please Euan."

Chapter 18

Euan knew exactly where to look for Billy Donnelly and that was in the pub. Judging by Nancy's telling of the sorry tale, he doubted if he would have gone home from the mill after his Saturday shift had finished and with money in his pocket he would now be drowning his sorrows.

At the third pub Euan visited he found him. His head down and a pint and an empty nip glass in front of him. Euan came up behind him and leaned into his ear. "I think we need a word Mr Donnelly," he said, while at the same time grasping him firmly by the elbow.

He felt Billy flinch.

"Have you not been expecting a visit from the law," Euan added, swiftly, "considering the activity you've been indulging in?"

Billy went to grasp the pint of beer but Euan stopped him.

"Outside," he said through gritted teeth. His dislike of the man was beginning to colour his judgement as a policeman. But Billy stood away from the bar and allowed Euan to walk him outside, much to the amusement of the other patrons, who were nudging and winking at one another as the pair left, before returning to the serious business of drinking their wages away.

"Where are we goin'?" Billy asked as he was propelled up King Street by the strong arm of the law.

"Home," was all Euan replied.

Once inside Billy's house in Victoria Road, Euan removed his tunic and turned to the young man. The blow he landed in Billy's stomach was not expected and he gasped and bent double as the wind was knocked out of him. He raised his head to plead ignorance with the policeman and as he did so, the second blow caught him high on the cheekbone just below his right eye.

He'd have a guid keeker the morn, Euan knew, which would serve as a reminder for days to come.

Billy collapsed into a chair, the nausea in his stomach competing with the throbbing in his face.

"No more," he gasped, "I get the message."

Euan replaced his tunic and sat down opposite the man.

"It's been a wee while since me and Billy Dawson had to talk to you about being a man, but it looks like it fell on deaf ears. So, I'll say it again, you've a wife and twa bairns to your name now and if I find oot you've been at it again wi' a prostitute, it'll no' be just me that comes for you, it'll be Billy Dawson as well."

Much to Euan's satisfaction, Billy's eye was beginning to close and swell.

"I'm going to fetch your family now," he said firmly, "so get yourself cleaned up and your story straight. You don't deserve a second chance with Nancy, but I'm not letting you desert her and the bairns with all the pain that would bring her. God knows why, but she seems to love you, so you'd better start loving her back. UNDERSTAND."

Euan towered over Billy as he stood up.

Billy nodded dismally.

"And Billy," Euan added, "let that black eye be a reminder of the trouble I can bring to you if you stray again."

Nancy was still reverberating from the thought of what Billy had been up to when Euan returned.

Before Annie could ask him anything, he began to put Mary Anne's coat on her and held out Nancy's. "Time to go home," he said kindly, "I've spoken with Billy and I think there's been a bit of a misunderstanding."

"Misunderstanding?" Nancy echoed.

Annie looked confused but said nothing.

"Come on," continued Euan brooking no argument, "I'll come with you and make sure you get home alright."

The suddenness and decisiveness of Euan's actions left Nancy with no option but to obey and together with her children, she was returned home to face her husband and the future.

Annie was still stunned when Euan returned.

"What happened?"

"Nothing for you to worry about," he said, "just let's say that I don't think Billy Donnelly will be giving Nancy any more grief."

Once again, Annie was struck by the way her husband seemed to be able to deal with things and fleetingly thought that finding out about her and Billy Dawson's son might not be the end of their lives together.

Lexie had been into town, aimlessly wandering from shop to shop, hoping against hope that somehow Robbie would find her again. Things with Charlie were going from bad to worse, as he ran out of ideas to bring back the smile on Lexie's face and Lexie gave him only cursory attention when he was around anyway.

She wished at times she'd never met Robbie again, but having felt the emotional depth of her attraction to him, there seemed nothing she could do to put him out of her mind.

On her return home and wishing she could cancel Charlie's usual Saturday night visit, she was unprepared for Annie's revelation that Robbie Robertson had accosted her in the butcher's the day before. What was he playing at? And why did he leave her standing outside the park gates waiting for him when he knew how much she'd wanted to see him.

It had taken all her skills at subterfuge to convince her mother that she'd no idea what she was talking about and even more skill to keep her from telling Charlie.

Using the excuse to go to her bedroom to get changed for Charlie's arrival, Lexie hurried out of the kitchen.

This was no use, she told herself. Either she had to forget about Robbie Robertson and deny her feelings for him or, at least, tell Charlie their secret engagement was off. But one way or another, something had to be done, she couldn't bear to feel this way much longer.

Charlie turned up around seven and suggested they go to the pictures, as usual. He was hoping Lexie's off hand behaviour towards him would stop soon, but quickly realised that, if anything, it had become worse.

Lexie's stomach was awash with butterflies. "I fancy a walk," she announced, moving towards the parlour door, without waiting for an answer, "I'll get my coat."

Charlie shrugged at Annie and Euan and followed her out.

But, it was Charlie who started to speak.

"I don't know if it's me or what, but is something wrong... between us I mean?"

The opportunity had presented itself for Lexie to call off their engagement but instead she answered with a 'no'.

Charlie's breathing eased. "So, what's wrong then?" he asked.

Lexie sighed. "I suppose," she began, "that I'm fed up just being engaged," and before she could stop herself she began rambling on about how it would be better if they were married.

That would stop her thinking about Robbie Robertson, she told herself. She'd be married to Charlie and that would be that. Then Robbie Robertson would be sorry, when he found out he'd missed his chance with her.

Charlie had stopped walking. "Do you mean it?" he asked, he'd started out worrying that Lexie was going to end it all and now she was talking about marrying him!

Lexie fretted. Why didn't Charlie just sweep her off her feet the way Robbie had done and make her his. Instead he was asking her if she meant what she said.

Suddenly frustrated by Charlie's lack of manliness and her longing for Robbie, she turned on him.

"Of course I didn't mean it," she shouted, turning heads in the street in their direction, "in fact," she added fiercely, "I don't ever want to see you again."

Charlie stood in stunned silence as Lexie turned and walked away.

He had never felt so lost. What was he supposed to do now? Chase after her, leave her alone, go home. He needed time to think about what had just happened and that's when Charlie made his mistake. Charlie went home.

Chapter 19

Sarah was having the most beautiful day of her life. John Adams had come into the library, as he'd promised, and made a bee line for her. Both of them, but especially John, were unsure of their ground, but he grasped the nettle.

"I've noticed there's a teashop round the corner in Meadowside," he began, a bit nervously, "so if you'd like to join me for..."

Before he could finish the sentence Sarah nodded vigorously. "I'd love to," she said, happily.

John broke into a grin at Sarah's enthusiastic response. "Right," he said, "I'll just return this medical book and we can go... if that's alright with you?"

"It's very alright with me," she said, looking towards the door. "I'll wait for you outside on the steps."

What a wonderful day, Sarah thought, as she stood at the top of the curved stairway, the sun was shining, the sky was blue and even the statue of Rabbie Burns seemed less sombre. And, not only that, she was stepping out with the very handsome, very charming, soon to be a doctor, John Adams.

The teashop was busy, but the waitress found them a table in the corner which suited them both. Sarah looked round, matronly women took up much of the tables, their heads bobbing up and down, putting the world to rights as they sipped their tea.

Sarah giggled. "I think we're the youngest here," she said.

"They all look like my mum."

The waitress came over to their table.

"Whit can I get you twa then?" she asked, pencil poised over her small ordering pad.

"Tea," John asked Sarah, "and maybe some scones?"

"Perfect." Whatever John had suggested would have been perfect. She gazed at him as he placed their order and thanked the waitress.

"So," he began, "tell me about yourself?"

Sarah blushed. No man had ever been interested enough in her before to ask.

"Well," she said, trying to bring her thoughts together enough to say something exciting about herself, but failed. She wished she was Lexie Melville. She'd have known what to say and how to impress this man.

"I'm going to be a teacher." If she could have taken back the words, she would have, and replaced them with something flirty and feminine. The vision of a middle-aged spinster, like some of the women at her old school, filled her head. "At least, that's what mother wants me to be," she added quickly, "but maybe I won't," she finished lamely.

The waitress returned to their table with a tray laden with the tea things and a plate of scones. It seemed to Sarah it took forever for the girl to finally leave them alone again, but by this time, she was sure John would think her a frumpy, bookworm and the confidence she'd felt at the start of their meeting rapidly began draining away.

"Well isn't that just great," John said, "good for you. Most of the girls I meet back home just want to get married and have babies."

Sarah could have cried. That's what she wanted too, only her mother had other plans for her which she had always felt powerless to rebel against.

There was a marked lull in the conversation while Sarah poured the tea and John buttered his scone. Sarah felt that things weren't going well. Maybe John had already met someone back in Ireland and she was just a bit of amusement till he returned home. The thought depressed her, for the first time in her life she had met someone she was attracted to and maybe it was already too late.

"And, what about you," she finally managed to ask him, hoping there would be no mention of a girlfriend back home, "being a doctor must keep you very busy?"

John laughed, "I'm not a doctor yet," he said, "I've another two years after this one before I qualify, that's if I qualify."

Sarah began to get her confidence back. "Oh, I'm sure you will," she said, "and I think you'll make a wonderful doctor."

John grinned and raised his teacup in acknowledgement of the compliment, "And I think you'll make a wonderful teacher."

Sarah beamed with pleasure, it was alright, he didn't think she was an old frump and maybe, just maybe, he actually liked her too.

The best day of Sarah's life concluded with her returning to the library to finish her duties for the day while John made his way back to the hospital, but not before arranging to meet her again the following week, same time, same place, he'd said and Sarah had happily agreed.

When the library closed, Sarah walked on air all the way home. She must tell Lexie about her wonderful day with John Adams and that they were going to meet again. This was much more exciting than Lexie's encounter with Robbie Robertson and it was with a spring in her step and a glow in her heart that she returned home.

But Josie was waiting for her and by the expression on her face she wasn't pleased about something.

Sarah felt herself cringe inside as her mother's gaze seemed to look right through her.

"Had a good day at the library?" Josie asked.

Sarah looked at the faces of her two sisters searching for some explanation to justify the cold atmosphere.

"Well," Josie continued, "I'm waiting."

Sarah's mind began to race. Her mother couldn't possibly know about John Adams, no one knew, except Lexie, of course, and she felt sure she wouldn't have said anything.

"It was fine," Sarah eventually said, "busy, but fine."

"So," her mother said slowly, "you never met anyone there, no one from Ireland for example?"

A real fear was now forming in Sarah's stomach. She could only mean John Adams, but how did she know about him!

Her mind went completely blank.

"Well?" again her mother pushed for an answer.

There was no point in denying it, somehow, Josie knew about John Adams.

Taking a very deep breath, Sarah faced her mother. "As a matter of fact," she began, trying to control the tremor in her voice, "I did meet someone there and we went for tea at the cafe in Meadowside."

There it was out.

"So, it's true what I've heard," Josie stated, "you've been wasting your time with some man when you should have been studying. Have you completely lost your senses?"

Sarah felt tears filling her eyes. "I wasn't wasting my time," she cried, "and he isn't 'some man', his name is John Adams and he's going to be a doctor and I like him."

Josie tensed. This was worse than she'd been led to believe by Annie Melville. This John Adams was a real danger to her plans for Sarah's future and she had to put a stop to it.

"Well, that's as maybe," she said, "but I can't trust you anymore to behave like a lady and not go throwing yourself at anything in trousers, so you won't be going to the library anymore."

It was at that moment that Billy Dawson entered his home to be met by a wall of silence. He looked from Josie to Sarah and back again, taking in the set determination of his wife's mouth and the tearful face of his daughter.

"What's all this then," he asked quietly?

"Ask your daughter?"

Sarah shook her head and ran from the room.

Billy looked at Josie and waited for an explanation.

"We need to talk about Sarah," Josie said, grimly, "but not in front of the girls," she added indicating the two younger sisters sitting goggle eyed on the sofa.

Billy inclined his head towards the door and with much nudging and winking, his daughters left the room.

Josie sat down and Billy followed suit. "This looks serious," he said, lighting a cigarette and trying not to outguess his wife, "maybe you should start at the beginning and tell me what Sarah's been up to."

Sarah was his first born daughter and his favourite, but Josie was her mother and he always made sure that her decisions about Sarah were supported by him.

"I've had a visit from Annie Melville," she began. Billy flinched, if Annie was involved, then Josie was always going to see the worst of it.

"And," she continued, "she came to tell me something about Sarah and a man." Josie let the statement hang in the air between them.

Billy frowned. "A man," he repeated, "what man is this then?"

Josie began to warm to her news. "According to Annie Melville, Sarah has met a man at the Reference Library and it looks like she's had her head turned by him. His name's John Adams and he's an Irishman over here for some sort of exchange visit."

Billy let the information settle in his head.

"She's seventeen now Josie," he said, "you must have known that sooner or later she was going to meet someone..." but Billy got no further.

"Of course," she rounded angrily, "you're always going to take Sarah's side, even when it's going to ruin her future..." Tears of frustration began to flow down her face.

So that was it, he realised, stubbing out his cigarette in the ashtray and lighting another, Sarah had met a young man and Josie feared that her dreams of her daughter becoming a teacher had just shattered.

"Hey, hey," he said, joining Josie on the sofa.

"Has Sarah said she doesn't want to be a teacher then?"

Josie shook her head.

"Well then," continued Billy, keeping his voice calm, "this all sounds like something and nothing and when this John Adams goes back to Ireland, it will all be forgotten and Sarah will go to the University and get her degree and become a teacher, just like you want."

"I've told her she can't go back to the library," Josie added, feeling a bit more reassured. "Maybe, you could go instead and just make sure this man knows that Sarah's not that kind of girl and..."

Billy hushed his wife. "Let me speak to Sarah first," he said, "and then we'll decide what's best."

With Josie placated, Billy went through to his daughter's bedroom to find her staring out of the window at nothing in particular.

He pulled up the basket chair and sat alongside her.

"Mum's in a bit of a state," he said, taking her hand and willing her to look at him.

Sarah nodded glumly. "John and me just had tea and scones together," she said, "that's all."

Billy acknowledged her innocence.

"And you like him?"

"Yes."

"And do you expect to see him again?"

Sarah's eyes brightened. Her father was always so understanding and she just knew it would be alright if he was on her side.

"Next Wednesday," she said, "but mum says I'm not to go back to the library ever again..."

Billy hushed his daughter. "How would it be if I went instead and had a word with the man, with John I mean and explained things a bit and maybe by then your mother will have calmed down and accepted that seeing this young man now and then, isn't going to stop you from doing your degree and becoming a teacher."

Sarah brightened some more and spontaneously she threw her arms around her father. "He's really nice," she babbled, "and he's Irish, just like you and he's a real gentleman..."

Billy unwrapped himself from his daughter's arms.

"I think I've got the message," he said, smiling. But Billy Dawson had realised that, this time, Josie was right and this young man could truly jeopardise Sarah's future.

He would have to make sure John Adams had no place in his daughter's future.

Chapter 20

Annie's visit to Josie Dawson had gone well. She knew there was no love lost between herself and Josie and that the past would always be an issue for her. Despite being married to Billy and bearing three daughters to him, she still saw Annie as her rival for Billy's love and Annie knew for certain that the appearance of her and Billy's son would destroy Josie and her family completely.

"So, I don't know how far things have gone," she'd said to Josie, "but I felt it my duty to let you know about Sarah and this young man."

Josie had listened to Annie, her temper threatening to erupt in front of her nemesis, as she imparted the news of her daughter's secret tryst.

"Well," she'd said tightly to Annie, "I'm thankful for your letting me know about this man Mrs Melville and I'll certainly be speaking to Sarah about it soon."

She'd shown Annie the door, without offering her tea, but it was with a deep sigh of relief that Annie returned home. Josie was not a woman to cross, especially when it came to her eldest daughter and she felt sure, she would put a stop to the romance before things got any more serious.

Annie met the day of her next meeting with her son at the Howff with a light mood. Apart from Lexie still mooning about the place, which had worsened since Charlie's departure, things felt calm and Annie was allowing herself to think that her son's stay in Dundee would go undiscovered and that all would return to normal in a few months' time.

Careful this time to make sure that Constable O'Rourke was nowhere around, she made her way into the cemetery. She was the first to arrive and, like before, seated herself on the low gravestone at the back of the Howff. It was some time before John turned up and Annie was beginning to think something had happened to him when she saw his dark hair and handsome face seeking her out.

"Over here," she called waving a gloved hand.

John hurried towards her. "Sorry," he said, "a bit of an emergency at the hospital, so everyone was called in to help, even me."

Annie unpacked the basket and handed her son a sandwich before unscrewing the flask of hot tea.

"You look as though you need this," she said, noticing the bleak look in his eyes.

John took the tea. "Thanks mum," he said. Annie loved it when he called her 'mum'.

"But that's not what's bringing me down."

Annie bit into her own sandwich, watching her son closely.

Since her visit to Josie Dawson, she'd heard nothing about Sarah and Lexie wasn't in any frame of mind to tell her anything more, even if there was any more to tell that is.

"Do you remember that girl I told you about, Sarah?"

Annie nodded, her sandwich forgotten.

"Well, she and I were supposed to meet again last week, but she didn't turn up."

Annie began eating again, Josie had done her work.

She feigned concern. "I'm sorry John," she said, "and you really liked her too."

"Not only that," he continued, chewing on the last bit of his sandwich, "her father turned up instead. To warn me off!"

Annie almost choked on the bread. Billy Dawson had come face to face with his son!

John rushed to Annie's aid, slapping her back till she spat out the bread and began to breathe again.

"Are you alright?" he asked anxiously. "I didn't mean to startle you."

Annie calmed herself down. "No, no," she spluttered, "I'm fine."

Wiping tears from her eyes and dabbing her face with her handkerchief, she asked, shakily, "And what did he say to you?"

John shrugged.

"Not a lot really," he told her, "just that Sarah was going to University soon to become a teacher and that now wasn't a good time for her to be getting involved with men."

Annie began to relax.

"I told him we were just friends and that's all, but he would have none of it and I haven't seen her since."

Annie was genuinely sorry now for her son, but the truth would have been much worse to hear if the romance had blossomed.

"And what did you think of her father then?" Annie couldn't stop herself from asking.

"He was alright, I suppose," John said, "but I wouldn't want to get on the wrong side of him," he added, "big old man that he is."

For John's sake, Annie wanted to tell her son the truth. That he had met his real father, but now it was impossible for that to happen and Annie was glad. Maybe someday in the future, she would write to him and explain, but now wasn't the time.

They parted on good form, with John kissing her on both cheeks before heading off to the Infirmary again and Annie making off in the opposite direction. But it wasn't Constable O'Rourke that saw her this time, it was Sarah Dawson, who couldn't understand what Mrs Melville was doing being kissed on the cheek by John Adams.

She needed to speak to Lexie. She'd know what this was all about. And had Lexie's mother anything to do with her being 'found out'?

Sarah had visited the library every day since her mother had ordered her not to, but she hadn't actually gone in, just stood nearby, so in her obedient mind, that was alright. Her fingers had been firmly crossed that John would somehow see her, so she could explain things to him, but he'd never turned up, not till today that is, and in the company of Mrs Melville!

Not wanting to go to Lexie's home, she decided to wait for her outside Baxters office and find out what this was all about.

She watched as the workers from the Calender streamed out of the loading bay and then the glass doors of the offices next door opened to release the office staff back to their lives outside work.

Lexie was one of the first out and Sarah hurried across the road to join her.

Even in her depressed state, Lexie was pleased to see her friend. Maybe she had news of Robbie, she thought, but the forlorn hope was dashed when Sarah announced that she'd seen Mrs Melville in town earlier, with a young man.

Lexie was perplexed. "What are you talking about Sarah," she asked?

Sarah linked her arm into Lexie's. "I'll tell you on the tram," she said, as the girls crossed the road to the tram stop.

Once they were settled into their seats, Sarah began her story.

"First of all," she said, "I owe you an apology."

Lexie became more confused. "What for?"

"Well, I thought you'd told my mum about me and John Adams…"

Lexie cringed. She'd been found out and began to try to think of excuses why she'd betrayed her friend's confidence to her mother.

"But now I know it wasn't you at all."

"Oh!" exclaimed Lexie, getting interested. "Then who was it?"

"It was your mum."

Lexie couldn't believe her ears. Her mother had told Josie Dawson about her daughter's secret love. How could she!

Sarah could see the look of horror in Lexie's eyes. "No," she said quickly, "that's what I'm trying to tell you. Your mum knows John Adams. I saw him kissing her goodbye outside the Howff today."

By the look on Lexie's face, Sarah knew that this was also news to her.

"Are you sure?"

Sarah nodded. "So, maybe when my mum knows that Mrs Melville is a friend of John's she'll be alright with me seeing him."

But Lexie wasn't listening anymore. She needed some answers and the only one who could supply them, was her mother.

Chapter 21

By the time Euan had returned Nancy and the little ones back to their house in Victoria Road, Billy had cleaned up the tiny house and himself. He'd found clean sheets and made up the bed and opened the window wide to let in a blast of fresh air.

His eye was now almost fully closed, and turning blacker by the minute, but his mind was on trying to concoct a story convincing enough for Nancy to believe him.

He opened the door to Euan's knock.

"Here they are then Billy," Euan said, ushering Nancy and the bairns forward, "home safe and sound."

He swept Mary Anne into his arms and guided Nancy and wee Billy into the kitchen.

"Nasty eye you've got there," said Euan, pointedly, when Nancy was just out of earshot, "have a wee accident?"

Nancy looked round at her husband. "Something like that," he said, trying to close the door, but Euan's foot prevented it from closing.

"Last chance, remember," Euan whispered, tapping the side of his nose, "I'll give Billy Dawson your regards the next time I see him."

Billy nodded dismally and turned to face his wife.

"The kettle's boiled," he said, helping Nancy off with her coat before she could change her mind about staying.

Nancy watched as he made the tea and brought the cups to the table, the look on her face suggesting that he had some explaining to do and he'd better do it quickly.

"I'm sorry Nancy, to you and to the bairns," he began, never looking at his wife, but staring instead at the teacup. "I know what it looks like, but you're wrong... about everything."

Nancy raised an eyebrow and waited. The look on the face of her fellow washer, was etched into her mind and the words she had used to justify her disgust, ate away at her.

"Do you remember when wee Billy was born," he asked, bleakly?

Nancy said nothing and remained unmoved.

"Well," he ploughed on, "Dr Finlayson was worried that if you fell again..." he hesitated then looked up at her, his eyes begging understanding. A tremor came into his voice and Nancy was unsure whether it was genuine or that another lie was coming.

He looked away again. "The doctor was worried that if you fell pregnant again, it might kill you."

"So, that's why you went whoring!" Nancy spat back.

"No, No," Billy tried to reach out for her hand but she pulled it away. "It wasn't like that, Nancy, you've got to believe me."

There were tears in his eyes now. "I was scared to love you, Nancy, like I wanted to..." He watched for her reaction, "in case I killed you."

The silence spread around the room like thick molasses.

"So, that's why you went whoring," Nancy repeated into the void that lay between them, her voice like ice.

Billy hung his head and slumped back into the chair. "Once," he said, hoarsely, "I went whoring, once." Now it was Billy who waited.

It didn't take long for Nancy to decide his fate. She could never trust Billy again, she knew that, but she also knew that without him and the money he brought in, her bairns would suffer dreadfully.

"I'll stay," she said firmly, "not for your sake, but for the bairns."

She steeled herself to continue. "I don't love you anymore Billy Donnelly, so you can stop worrying about any more of your seed coming into this world and I'll expect your full wages on the table every Friday, without fail."

Billy felt himself crumble inside. "Anything you say, Nancy," he said, "and if you'll let me, I'll make you love me again, just like you used to."

Nancy stood and looked around her home, it wasn't much but it was all she had and she'd make it a home for the bairns and herself and as for her husband, he could go to Hell.

Chapter 22

Lexie waved Sarah goodbye and tried to think of a way to ask her mother about John Adams. It must just be a case of mistaken identity she decided, her mother didn't know any young men and certainly none well enough for them to kiss her!

Annie was in the kitchen as usual, preparing their supper and singing to herself. Lexie frowned. Her mother seemed happy, happier than usual, that is, and singing?

Lexie edged into the kitchen, still unable to believe Sarah's news.

"Need a hand," she asked, casually?

Annie turned to her daughter. It had been a long time now since Lexie had volunteered to help her in the kitchen. Maybe she was getting over her fractured courtship with Charlie, Annie surmised, or even putting the dreaded Robbie Robertson out of her mind at last.

"Wouldn't mind a hand with the shelling," she said, handing Lexie a bag of peapods and a bowl. Lexie sat at the kitchen table and bent to the task. She couldn't talk to her mother about John Adams, she decided, not without mentioning her own guilt at speaking to Annie about him. She'd speak to Euan, she finally decided, sure that he'd know about this John Adams and why he was kissing her mother in the street.

And what was all the fuss about anyway, she pondered. Just because Sarah had met a man, surely she was seventeen now, and able to do what she wanted? But Lexie knew Sarah's mother and could imagine her reaction at the news that her precious daughter was interested in anything other than being a teacher.

The peas shelled, Lexie excused herself and went to her bedroom to consider her options. She could say nothing and let the silly episode be forgotten; she could ask her mother outright about John Adams; or she could try to get to the bottom of this by tackling Euan.

The front door opened and closed and she could hear Euan hang his tunic and helmet on the hallstand and exchange his boots for his slippers. She could hear his voice as he went into the kitchen, telling Annie he was home. He sounded normal, in fact, everyone seemed normal except her that is, as she painted picture after picture of John Adams kissing her mother.

Ian rushed past her into the kitchen, following the aroma of food cooking and plonked himself down onto one of the kitchen chairs, knife and fork at the ready. Yes, Lexie thought, taking her place at the table, even Ian was behaving normally, but still…

The meal was delicious, as usual, the conversation was minimal, as usual, as everyone tucked into their supper, but as the meal ended, Lexie took her chance.

"Had a good day, mum?" she asked, unsure of how she would respond to Annie's answer.

Her mother gave her a quizzical look. "Fine," she said, "thank you for asking."

But Lexie persisted. "Meet anyone special?"

Annie froze. "Matter of fact, I did," she said, her mind racing.

"Bumped into one of your old teachers," she lied, "Miss Malone."

Lexie knew then that her mother had something to hide. She would speak to Euan, and soon.

"How was she?"

Annie started to clear the table and turned her back on her family, her face beginning to burn with guilt. "She was fine, Lexie," she managed to reply, "happy to be retired."

Lexie had been acting strangely for so long now, Euan barely noticed the tension in her voice and as for his wife, he still didn't understand what was going on with her, but just hoped that it would all go away soon and things would go back to normal. But O'Rourke's report of Annie spending two hours in the church in the Nethergate niggled away at him and then there was the PC's accidental meeting with his wife outside the Howff, when she seemed, in his words, 'distracted', a word he'd been using himself lately to describe his wife's demeanour. But he hadn't bargained on Lexie and her news about the mysterious John Adams, when she'd asked to speak to him... privately.

There was nowhere private in the house where Lexie could speak to him 'privately' so he suggested they both go for a walk through Baxters Park, seeing as how the nights were getting shorter and the daylight lengthening.

With everything that had been happening, Annie smelled a rat. "We might join you," she said, lightly, "once I get the dishes put away."

But Euan put a finger to his lips to stop her going any further.

"I think Lexie wants to have a word about Charlie," he whispered, "looks like I might be recruited as the 'go between'. I think she misses him more that she's letting on." And with that, he quickly left the kitchen and Annie standing at the sink, while their son Ian doggedly ploughed through his homework at the table.

It was clear that Lexie had something she desperately wanted to divulge, but it wasn't till they were safely through the park gates and sitting on one of the benches that she told him.

"So," Lexie finished, "Sarah said she saw this young man that she's keen on, called John Adams, KISSING mum outside the Howff. WHO IS HE?" she asked desperately.

Euan let the information sink in. So, Annie was seeing someone after all and a much younger man at that! Euan felt shaken to the core, his mind going into overdrive. Surely, not 'a man of the cloth', he thought fearfully, remembering the two hours O'Rourke had said she'd spent in the Nethergate Church, but then there was the incident at the Howff with O'Rourke and now, the sighting by Sarah, of his wife kissing a man outside the Howff gates.

The controlled policeman inside him took over.

"Leave it with me, Lexie," he said. "I'm sure it's nothing you should be worrying your little head about. I'll speak to your mother later and we'll get it sorted out."

Now Lexie was even more worried, Euan didn't know anything about John Adams either!

"But what about you and Charlie then," Euan asked, changing the subject and seeking an update on Lexie's troubled love life. He'd need to have an answer for Annie when she surely asked about the 'private' meeting.

All thoughts of John Adams swiftly left Lexie's heart as they were replaced by images of Robbie Robertson.

"There is no Charlie," she said flatly.

Euan looked at his step-daughter. "So what's amiss then Lexie?"

He could see by the bleakness that now filled her eyes that she was very unhappy.

"He wasn't man enough for me," she said, "but Robbie Robertson is."

Euan could hardly believe his ears. What on earth had Robbie Robertson to do with anything, surely he'd been a 'bad lot' who'd almost led Lexie astray with that silly engagement ring of his?

"Robbie Robertson," Euan repeated. "But I thought that was all over long ago…"

"It was," replied Lexie, "but that was long ago and this is now." She turned with pleading eyes on Euan. "He's different now," she said, a softness coming into her voice, "he's been away at sea, in the Merchant Navy and he's come back changed."

"Changed?" Euan asked.

"He's come back a man," Lexie whispered almost to herself, "and I love him."

For the second time that evening, Lexie's news stunned Euan.

Robbie Robertson of all people, back into Lexie's life and now she says she loves him!

"And where is Robbie now?" Euan asked, almost sternly, determined to find him and speak to him about his re-entrance into Lexie's life and the misery it was obviously causing.

Lexie shrugged. "At sea, I suppose," she said, "we were supposed to meet but he never turned up." Her eyes searched Euan's face for an answer and he could hear the longing in her voice.

Euan remembered Robbie's ability to disguise the truth when he'd confronted him about the engagement ring. He'd seemed 'shifty' then and Euan knew from experience that leopards don't change their spots. He felt an anger rising as he wondered if he was manipulating his daughter again.

"C'mon," he said, helping Lexie up from the bench, "let's go home and sleep on it. Fate has a way of sorting things out you know," he counselled, "and it's usually for the best." But he didn't know how fate was going to handle the conversation he was going to have with Annie, once Lexie and Ian were asleep in their beds.

Chapter 23

"What do you mean, she knows him?" Josie asked Sarah, looking at her husband for an explanation.

Billy shook his head in ignorance. He'd spoken with the young man, warned him off and thought that was the end of it.

"But, it's true," Sarah insisted, "he was kissing her goodbye or something, outside the Howff Cemetery, so she must know him and if he's a friend of Mrs Melville, surely it's alright for me to be his friend too?"

"Annie Melville again," she said bitterness creeping into her voice, "is that woman always going to be interfering in our lives?" Billy could hear her voice rising.

"Calm down Josie," he said, as he saw Sarah begin to crumble at the wave of anger that was heading her way.

"Go to your room Sarah," he said quietly, "mum and me will get this sorted out."

Sarah's eyes glittered with tears, but she knew she couldn't stand up to her mother and ran from the room.

"I'll get us a cup of tea," he said to his smouldering wife, moving towards the kitchen and buying time to think of how to tackle this latest problem with his daughter. But finding out that Annie knew the young man and enough to let him kiss her in the street, filled him with a tension all of its own. He'd have to tread carefully, or Josie would turn the whole thing round on him and her fear of Annie Melville and their past.

He brought the tea through placing a cup on the small table next to Josie and lit a cigarette.

Josie posed the first question. "How does she know him?"

Then the second question. "Who is he?"

Then another, "And why was he kissing her and in the street?"

Josie tutted, indicating her intense dislike of Annie Melville.

Billy inhaled deeply on the cigarette. "Didn't she say she knew him when she told you about him and Sarah?"

Josie considered this. "No," she replied, "she didn't."

"Then if she does know him, why didn't she mention it at the time?"

There were more questions than answers, but Josie just knew there was something underhand going on with Annie Melville, she just didn't know what and neither did Billy Dawson.

"Whatever the reason why she knows him, doesn't alter the fact that I forbid Sarah to see him again."

As usual, Josie was taking a stand in ensuring Sarah's future of being a teacher, without ever asking her daughter what she wanted. She brushed aside any further discussion with Billy, she was going to find out herself about John Adams and the person to ask was Annie Melville herself.

Annie had been on tenterhooks since Euan and Lexie went for their walk. Was this 'private' talk really about building a bridge back to Charlie? Or, as she feared, since Lexie's question about meeting someone, it was something worse.

She didn't have long to wait. The sound of the returning pair reached her ears and she quickly picked up her knitting.

Euan came into the parlour but Lexie had gone straight to her room and without preamble, he confronted Annie.

"Your daughter's worried about you," he said, sitting down in his armchair, "and so am I."

Annie looked up from her knitting. Any hope of avoiding awkward questions faded, as she saw the look of hurt and disbelief on her husband's face.

She put down her knitting, she knew now this wasn't about Charlie but about her. "What's worrying you both then?" Annie asked trying to keep calm.

Euan sat forward in his chair and held Annie's gaze. "You've been seen," Euan began, "with a man."

"Really," Annie countered shakily, "and who might this man be?"

Euan sat back. "I was hoping you'd tell me that."

Annie felt there was no escape, Euan had to be told all about John Adams, her illegitimate son.

"It's true," she said, "I have been seeing another man." Euan felt his whole world crumble. "But, it's not what you think," she added hastily.

"There's something you need to know, Euan," Annie went on, determinedly, "but I don't want Lexie or Ian hearing what I'm about to tell you."

Euan waited, the anxiety in his system almost making him vomit.

Then Annie told her husband the whole sorry tale about the workhouse and the birth and how the nuns had taken her son from her to be adopted. She told him about the letter from Dr Adams and how her son had wanted to write to her. Euan listened without interruption, everything was falling into place now and he could have wept with relief.

"And now," she said finally, "he's in Dundee on an exchange scholarship for six months and I've met him three times, once at the church in the Nethergate and twice in the Howff Cemetery."

Annie stood up and straightened her shoulders. "I love him Euan," she stated emphatically, "so, if you want me to leave," she said, her chin now quivering with the strain, "then I'll understand." Suddenly, Euan too was on his feet and gathering her into his arms.

"Oh, Annie," he said, "I thought you'd met someone else and were planning to leave me!"

Annie couldn't believe her ears. Euan knew the truth about her past and still wanted her!

Tears of release began to flow as Euan held her. So, she'd had a child out of wedlock all these years ago in Ireland Euan now knew and the guilt had haunted her to this day. He turned her face towards him.

"It's alright Annie love," he said gently, "this changes nothing between us and, Annie, if you wish, I'd like to meet him."

Annie hugged her wonderful husband. "I think he'd like that too," she said, and meant it.

That night for the first time in a long time, Annie slept like a bairn.

She could trust Euan not to tell Lexie or Ian and maybe, in time, she'd also want them to know. But for now, knowing she had the love and support of Euan was enough.

He hadn't asked who John's father was and Annie had kept that detail to herself. Now, Billy Dawson would never need to know about his son and soon John would be going back to Ireland, after meeting Euan, of course.

Chapter 24

The atmosphere in the Donnelly household could be cut with a knife. Nancy busied herself with the house and bairns while Billy kept his head down and worked all the hours that he could, trying to buy back Nancy's love.

There had been no intimacy since her return and although they continued to share the same bed, there was a gulf between them that Billy couldn't bridge. Any time his thoughts turned to Gladys Kelly, which they often did, the memories of Sergeant MacPherson and Billy Dawson soon dispelled them. He knew only too well what would happen to him if he weakened and gave in to his lust.

Every morning he woke with the idea of just running away. Do what he'd always wanted to do and head for the hills, but the reality of his life soon replaced that thought as he braced himself for another day at the mill and his loveless life.

Breakfast was taken in silence as Nancy busied herself with the children, deliberately keeping them to herself and chiding Mary Anne when she'd toddle over to her father's side and stretch up her arms to him.

"Dada's got to go to work," she'd tell Mary Anne sharply, reaching for her with her free hand while the other arm cradled wee Billy.

This would often result in Billy leaving his breakfast half eaten and turning up at the mill early. It was Billy Dawson that noticed this and that morning, called out to him to come into the loading bay 'Buckie.'

"Why so early?" he asked, fearing that he'd been at Gladys Kelly's all night and hadn't been home.

Billy kicked the legs of a stool and sat down.

Would his father in law understand what his life was like? He doubted it.

"No reason," he said, "just woke early that's all."

Billy pursed his lips.

"And Nancy, how's Nancy and the little ones?"

Billy began to feel resentful. Nancy was just fine, it was him that needed understanding, but he knew he wouldn't get any from Billy Dawson.

"They're all fine," he said without feeling, "so if there's nothing else you want to know, then I'll get on with my work."

Billy eyed him suspiciously. Something was wrong but he could only surmise what it was.

"Keeping away from Gladys Kelly?" he asked, pointedly, now standing in front of the only exit out of the office.

Billy could feel his temper rising. "So, that's what you really want to know," he said through gritted teeth. "Sergeant MacPherson been talking, has he?"

It was only when the words were out that he realised that Billy knew nothing of his encounter with the policeman.

Billy grew quiet. "No," he said slowly, "I haven't spoken to Euan MacPherson for some time now, so maybe you can tell me what the big secret is."

It wasn't a question, it was a demand and Billy felt trapped.

His mind was racing. He had to think of an answer quickly and get out of this place and away from Billy Dawson, before he got any deeper into trouble.

"I got drunk," he said, "that's all."

Billy didn't take his eyes off the young man.

"Is it?"

"If you don't believe me, why don't you ask him yourself," Billy rounded boldly. "I'm sure he'll tell all."

Billy stepped away from the door.

"Oh, I'll ask him alright and if I find you've been lying..." He let the words hang in the air as he opened the door for Billy to escape.

Without another word, Billy fled to the sanctuary of the Calender.

His muscles were like bow strings and his mind was fearful.

He couldn't keep living like this, he decided, everywhere he turned there was nothing but hatred and distrust and he felt even his God had truly deserted him. Billy never felt so alone.

He worked relentlessly till the bummer sounded the end of the shift, the effort helping to ease the tension in his body. There was nowhere to go but home and his feet dragged him up William Lane and onto Victoria Road. There had to be a way to make life better, but he couldn't think of it as went in through the door of his miserable existence.

Nancy met him with a worried look in her eyes. "It's wee Billy," she said, anxiously, "he's been coughing all day and his nose is running like water from the well." Billy went over and felt his son's brow, he was warm, but not hot.

"It's probably just the sniffles," he said, trying to sound reassuring, but Nancy wasn't convinced.

"But he hasn't eaten all day," she said, "and the cough is getting worse." He was glad that Nancy was now speaking to him, although it was for all the wrong reasons.

"Go, get Auntie Annie," she said fearfully, "she'll know what to do."

Billy didn't argue. Nancy was really worried. He pulled his jacket back on and took hold of Nancy's shoulders. "I'll be back before you know it," he said, "don't worry."

For the first time, Nancy didn't push him away, glad that he was with her and the bairns. She nodded and allowed herself to rest against him for a few seconds before letting him go.

Billy almost ran to Annie's house in Albert Street. It didn't matter that Sergeant MacPherson might be there, he just needed to bring Annie back with him. But Euan MacPherson was there and could see at once that Billy was panicking.

"Is Mrs MacPherson in?" he asked Euan breathlessly, "Nancy needs her."

Annie came to the door to find out what all the fuss was about.

Whenever Billy saw her, he pulled at her arm. "You need to come quickly," he said, "it's wee Billy, he's sick and Nancy's worried it's something bad."

Euan handed Annie her coat and put on his tunic. "I'm coming too," he told her quietly, "you don't have to do everything on your own anymore."

Annie nodded, she knew what he meant and capable as she was, his support gave her extra strength.

The minute Annie entered the little house and heard the child's cough, she knew. "Whooping Cough," she said to Euan decisively.

She hugged her niece and went to the crib. Wee Billy was getting distressed and his breathing was shallow. "He needs to go to hospital Nancy," she said, her practical side taking over, "and quickly."

Euan stepped in. "I'll get onto the station," he said, "there's a police box across the road at Wellington Street. I'll get them to send a motor right away."

Euan hurried from the kitchen and Nancy carefully lifted her son into her arms. Billy rushed to her side, the sight of Nancy and wee Billy in such distress, making him determined to show his family his love for them and never to hurt any of them again.

Annie took Mary Anne's hand and the little group made their way down into the street. "It won't be long," she said to Billy, who was looking pale and fearful, "and wee Billy will be in good hands at the Infirmary."

The black van pulled up at the kerb and they all got into the back.

Euan sat in front with the driver and instructed him to go as fast as he could to the DRI.

Things move fast once they arrived at the hospital, with a nursing sister immediately taking the infant from Nancy. "Wait here," she said, "the duty doctor will see him at once."

Euan and Annie, Nancy and Billy all filed into the dark waiting room at the entrance to the Infirmary and waited, no one wishing to talk but all fearing the worst.

It was an hour later that the door of the waiting room opened and the doctor in his white coat with a stethoscope around his neck came in.

"Mr and Mrs Donnelly," he said, seeking out the couple in the gloom, "I'm Dr Adams, it's about your son, Billy?"

Annie couldn't believe her eyes. Her son stood before her.

"John?"

John Adams turned and peered into the corner of the room.

What was his mother doing here with the parents of this sick child. Confused, he turned back towards Nancy and Billy and ushered them out of the room. "Dr Whitelaw wishes to speak to you," he told them gently, "he's the Infirmary's doctor for the children."

Both Euan and Annie sat very still while Mary Anne slept on Euan's lap.

"Was that him?" Euan finally asked.

Annie nodded. This wasn't how she'd planned the meeting of her son and Euan, but now that it had happened... fate had lent a hand again.

Euan had only seen the young man briefly, but was struck by his dark and handsome looks. Whoever the father was, he thought to himself, he must have been impressive.

A short time later, John came back into the waiting room, but before he could say anything, Annie pointed at Euan.

"It wasn't meant to be like this," she said, "but this is my husband Euan MacPherson and the child's mother is Nancy Donnelly, my late sister Mary's daughter."

John could hardly take it all in. All of a sudden, he had met his mother's husband and her niece. He shook Euan's free hand and smiled at Annie.

"I'm sorry we've met under these circumstances," he continued saying to both of them, "but the baby's in good hands. Dr Whitelaw is our child specialist and the best there is, so try not to worry." Annie felt immense pride at John's ability to ease their troubled minds and felt sure that wee Billy would be fine.

On Nancy and Billy's return, John nodded them goodbye and went back to the wards, while Annie fussed over her niece and the now wakened Mary Anne.

"He's being kept in," Billy explained to Euan, his mouth dry with fear. "They've put him in a thing called an oxygen tent to help him breathe and Dr Whitelaw says that the next few days will be critical." Billy pulled Euan aside. "If he dies," he whispered, "I'll never forgive myself."

Euan looked perplexed. "Why do you say that Billy?" he asked.

Billy looked at the ground. "It's the sins of the fathers, isn't it," he said fearfully, "I'm being punished for what I did with Gladys Kelly."

"Punished!" Euan echoed. He turned the young man to face him.

"Is this about your religion again?" he asked, incredulously.

In the midst of all that was happening, Billy had now added guilt onto his shoulders.

"I think it's time you stopped living your life to the rules of the Catholic Church," Euan said, trying to keep the anger out of his words, "and start living for your family and yourself instead."

He shook his head sadly and wondered at the power of the priests that made a young man live with so many rules that it was humanly impossible to cope with them.

"C'mon," he said, "let's get you all home. And Billy," Euan added, "this too will pass, just be strong and look after Nancy and Mary Anne."

The little group trooped back to their separate homes with Billy holding Nancy's hand all the way.

"Will they be alright?" Annie asked once they had returned home themselves and explained to Lexie and Ian what had happened.

"I hope so," said Euan, "for all their sakes."

In bed that night, Euan spoke of John Adams. "He's a very handsome lad, Annie," he said, "do you want to tell me who his father was?"

There was no hesitation. "He was an Irish labourer," she lied, "came to work at the farm for the flax harvest."

"Did he have a name?"

"No name, just called himself John."

True or not, Euan decided to accept Annie's answers. It all happened a long time ago in a faraway land, he decided. And with that thought, he closed his eyes and went to sleep.

"Goodnight Annie," he whispered.

"Goodnight Euan. Sleep tight."

Chapter 25

Now that Euan had been told about Annie's son, he could understand why Annie didn't want Lexie to know about him.

She was too young, she'd explained, maybe once she was married with bairns of her own, she'd be less likely to condemn her mother's past.

Euan had agreed, but still felt that Lexie had more on her mind than John Adams and talked Annie into leaving Lexie to him and to deal with Robbie Robertson and Charlie, if need be.

But Lexie had her own ideas about who she loved and had listened to Euan with only one ear while secretly planning her own future.

One way or another, she was going to find Robbie Robertson and tell him how she felt, this unrequited love was eating her up, even Mrs Fyffe had noticed the change in her demeanour, and it was now affecting her work.

"Lexie," she'd asked one day, "is anything wrong at home?"

Lexie tried to bring her attention back to the invoices she was filing in the General Office. Mrs Fyffe was always intuitive when it came to Lexie, especially since she'd taken up with her nephew Charlie Mathieson.

"Sorry, Mrs Fyffe," Lexie said, "just a bit tired, that's all."

But Mrs Fyffe wasn't buying it.

"The kettle's on," she said, kindly, "come and have a cup of tea in my office." She knew Billy Dawson had pushed Lexie, at her mother's asking, into working at Baxters offices, but she'd grown to really like the young girl and saw behind the confident front she always showed to the world, to the innocent lass underneath. But, she didn't expect to hear Lexie's news, when she'd asked her if anything was wrong.

"Me and Charlie have broken up," she told Mrs Fyffe bluntly.

The older woman flinched. Charlie had said nothing to her or, as far as she knew, to his family. They all thought that he and Lexie were together and even planning to become engaged.

Mrs Fyffe steadied herself. "Is it final?" she asked.

Lexie nodded. "And is there anyone else involved in the parting?"

Lexie looked up at Mrs Fyffe, her young eyes bleak and miserable.

Whatever was happening in her life, Mrs Fyffe pondered, it wasn't making Lexie very happy.

She hung her head and stared at her hands. "Yes."

"Do you want to tell me about it Lexie?" she asked gently.

"His name's Robbie and I've known him since school, but he's been at sea in the Merchant Navy for two years and well, we've met again…"

Her voice began to falter as her unhappiness at her longing for the man enveloped her. "And I can't help it," she hurried on before Mrs Fyffe could stop her, "I can't stop thinking about him and wanting him and… I don't love Charlie anymore, I love Robbie Robertson."

Tears of loss and disillusionment spilled onto her cheeks.

Mrs Fyffe waited till Lexie calmed down and poured her a cup of tea.

"Here," she said, "drink this." Lexie slowly sipped the sweet tea.

"And does Robbie know how you feel?"

"That's the problem Mrs Fyffe," Lexie said, "we were meant to meet but he didn't turn up and well, now he's gone back to sea and I don't know what to do anymore."

The tears came again.

Mrs Fyffe's heart went out to the girl. She knew how she felt. The love of her own life had been lost and she'd gone on to marry Mr Fyffe.

Bert was alright, she knew, but didn't make her feel the way Michael O'Brian had. Even after all this time, she would have given anything to see Michael O'Brian again.

"I understand, Lexie," she said, "but sometimes life doesn't always work out the way we want and we have to accept things as they are."

Lexie knew Mrs Fyffe was trying to help, but nothing she said could change the deep desire that had formed in her heart for Robbie Robertson. Only seeing him again would do that and she prayed nightly that he'd come back to her.

She felt a bit better having spoken to Mrs Fyffe, but it had changed nothing, not her decision to break up with Charlie, nor her longing for Robbie.

But Lexie wasn't going to have to wait much longer for Robbie Robertson. Two weeks later, while doing some Saturday shopping for her mother, she saw him. He was coming out of Wallace's Tearooms, his arm firmly around the shoulders of a giggling girl.

Lexie froze on the spot, her heart thudding in her chest and her legs turning to jelly as she watched.

Then he saw her and after whispering something to the girl, crossed the road towards her. "Lexie," he said, grinning, "fancy meeting you again."

Lexie felt she would die, there was so much adrenalin rushing through her system, she could hardly breathe.

"What's the matter," Robbie asked, "cat got your tongue?"

Lexie glanced at the girl waiting on the other side of the street then turned back to the 'love of her life.' Only this time, instead of the handsome, manly and captivating sailor she saw before, here was a scruffy, pockmarked individual with greasy hair and he smelled of sweat!

How she'd ever thought she loved Robbie Robertson, she couldn't begin to imagine. Lexie suddenly found her voice. "I think your girlfriend's getting anxious," she said, nodding in the direction of the fretting girl, "and I don't have time to hang around, my fiancée's waiting for me. Charlie Mathieson," she added, "I think you know him?"

Robbie Robertson's face twisted into a sneer.

"You'd better hurry up then, lassie, can't keep Charlie boy waitin'."

Lexie smiled, for the first time in a very long time she felt free.

All the longing and desire she'd had for this ugly man had disappeared, just as quickly as it had come upon her, but life for Lexie would never be the same again. She had truly grown up.

She watched as Robbie turned his back on her and crossed over to the girl, repositioning his arm around her shoulders before walking out of Lexie's life for good.

On her return with the messages, Euan noticed immediately the change in Lexie and wanted to know the reason why.

He breathed a sigh of relief on the news that Robbie Robertson no longer figured in her life and was 'no more' as she'd put it.

"And what about Charlie?" he asked, "is there a way back for him?"

Lexie smiled and shook her head.

"I may have got it wrong with Robbie," she said, "but it showed me that what me and Charlie had was wrong too." Euan listened to Lexie's grown up reasoning in astonishment. Where was the little girl he knew, gone now, he surmised, replaced by a young woman who now knew the difference between puppy love, real love and lusty desire. He'd be able to report back to Annie that Lexie was fine, until the next time she fell in love, that is.

Chapter 26

Wee Billy had been kept in hospital for another two weeks, till he was over the worst of his Whooping Cough and no longer infectious to Mary Anne. Billy Dawson had been distraught on hearing about the bairn and went to the Infirmary with Nancy and Billy after his shift finished, while Josie minded Mary Anne.

He now saw the difference in his son in law and how Nancy was once more responding to his attention. The dark cloud of wee Billy's illness had produced a silver lining and Billy hoped that the couple would now grow stronger together.

On his third visit to the hospital, John Adams was on duty.

"He's the young doctor whose been looking after wee Billy," Nancy told her father, as they approached the window that looked into the child's isolation room.

"Is he now," said Billy, seeing for the second time his daughter's 'friend.' "Maybe I should thank him for all his help."

Nancy nodded. "I think he'd like that," she said, turning her attention back to her husband and to the small window.

John Adams felt a shimmer of fear in his stomach at the sight of Billy Dawson approaching him, but Billy reached out his hand in friendship.

The two men shook hands.

"I just wanted to say thanks," Billy said, "for looking after the little one so well." His eyes took in the man's looks and manner. Sarah had taste, he thought, this young man was everything a father could wish for in a son in law.

"Are you a relative then?" John asked.

Billy nodded towards Nancy. "She's my daughter," he said, "and wee Billy's my grandson."

John relaxed. Sarah's dad seemed less threatening than the last time they'd met.

"Hopefully, he'll be discharged by the end of the week," John said, putting on his doctor's hat again, "but we were a bit worried for a while, him being just a baby."

Billy was warming more and more to John Adams. He would make a wonderful doctor, he realised, and Josie was all wrong about him. He would speak to her again about Sarah being allowed to befriend the man while he was in Scotland. He could see no harm in that and Sarah would still go to University and become a teacher, like Josie wanted.

"I'll tell Sarah we've spoken again," he said before turning to join Nancy and Billy, "I'm sure something can be worked out, if you still want her friendship, that is?" he queried.

John couldn't believe his ears. "Of course," he said smiling, "that would be just fine."

They shook hands again. Did he imagine it? But Billy felt he'd known John Adams before. He shook his head free from the silliness and joined his daughter.

"Doctor says he'll be home by the end of the week," he told her.

"Really!" she exclaimed, hugging her husband, before turning back to Billy.

"Thanks dad," she said, "for being there again."

"It's what dad's do," he said back, "isn't that right Billy?"

Billy Donnelly acknowledged the remark as an indication that he'd been forgiven. Now, he just had to forgive himself.

Once Billy and Nancy had collected Mary Anne and headed off back to Victoria Road, Billy sat down beside Josie.

"How's Sarah?" he asked.

Josie huffed. "Oh, she's still moping over that daft lad," she said, "never seen such a carry on."

"He was on duty at the Infirmary tonight," Billy said, "when we were visiting wee Billy."

Josie turned to her husband. "And," she said, "what of it?"

Billy hesitated. He was going to have to phrase things very carefully if he was going to get past Josie's armour plating.

"He saved wee Billy's life," he exaggerated, "I believe if it wasn't for his doctoring skills, things might have turned out differently."

Josie frowned. Why was Billy defending the man?

"Well, that's as maybe," she said, "but there's still no place for him in our Sarah's life."

This was going to be harder than Billy had counted on.

"And, anyway, if Annie Melville has anything to do with him, you can be sure it will lead to trouble."

There it was again. Josie always managed to bring Annie Melville's name into everything, Billy thought. And what was John Adams to Annie anyway. What had Sarah said? He tried to remember the words, 'that she'd seen him kissing Annie goodbye in the street?'

Billy gave up. He needed more information before he tried again to break Josie's resolve and the only one who had any answers was Annie Pepper. His mind drifted back to his first meeting with her and how he'd loved her and left her. How he wished he'd had the courage to marry her then. It could all have been so different.

Josie's voice broke into his thoughts.

"I'm for bed," she said, getting up from her chair and straightening the front of her dress. "Coming?"

"In a while," Billy said, "just have another cigarette, then I'll be up."

But Billy fell asleep in his chair and it was gone midnight before he finally climbed into bed beside Josie. He had a good life with his wife and three beautiful daughters, but still something was missing and he knew what it was. He made up his mind, that if Sarah really wanted to see John Adams again, he was going to make sure it happened, despite what Josie said. No daughter of his was going to suffer the loveless existence that he now lived.

Tomorrow he would go and see Annie Pepper and enlist her help.

"He was on a late shift at the mill," he told Josie, when she asked him about going to work the next day.

She kissed him goodbye and gathered her books together. "See you tonight then," she said, "pupils to teach."

The house finally was empty, his two youngest daughters off to school and Sarah to the University Library to read up on Shakespeare.

Keeping his fingers crossed and feeling strangely alive, he went to the phone box at the end of the road and dialled Bell Street Police Station. "Sergeant MacPherson, please," he said to the voice.

"I'll just get him," came the reply. Billy replaced the receiver.

Good, Euan was at the station and Annie would be in on her own.

He made his way down Albert Street and into the close where she lived. He could feel excitement building in his heart, he was doing something against Josie's wishes and the intrigue intensified his emotions. He told himself it was for his daughter's sake that he had to speak to Annie but he was also glad of the excuse to speak to her for himself. He also wanted to know how she knew John Adams.

He knocked at the door, removing his bonnet as he did so.

Would he be welcome? The door opened and there she was, flour on her apron and the smell of baking hitting his nostrils.

"Billy!" she exclaimed. Her unexpected visitor held up a hand.

"It's alright," he said, "there's nothing wrong, I just need to have a word with you about something."

Annie stood back and Billy entered. "Kitchen?" he asked.

Annie nodded. "Just baking some scones," she explained, indicating he should sit down, while she took a batch out of the oven and replaced them with the next one. Her mind ran through various reasons why Billy Dawson was in her kitchen while Euan was at work, but none of them made sense.

Billy watched as she made them some tea and finally joined him at the table.

"I need your help," he said, "or support more like."

Annie was confused. It had always been her asking for his help in the past.

"If I can help, you know I will," she said cautiously.

"It's about Sarah and this John Adams she's met."

"I thought Josie had put a stop to that," Annie said, tensing at the mention of her son's name by Billy.

"She had," he said, "and that's why I'm here. I think she's making a mistake about the man."

"Mistake," Annie repeated, "how so?" She lowered herself onto a chair and felt the first signs of panic in her chest.

"He was at the Infirmary when I visited wee Billy," he told her, "and I took time to speak to him, you know, thank him for looking after the bairn and I got to know him a little better."

Annie wondered where this was leading. Did Billy see images of himself as a young man in John Adams?

"And I think it would be fine for Sarah to be his friend while he's in Scotland, I just can't get Josie to agree with me."

Annie stood up and busied herself with the cooling scones, taking them from their tray and putting them on the rack.

"So, what makes you think I can help?" Her back was to Billy and she could feel his eyes burning into her neck.

"Well," Billy hesitated, unsure how to form the question he'd been wanting to ask since he'd been told about the kissing. "Well, Sarah seemed to think you knew him, the way you allowed him to kiss you in the street and all."

Annie closed her eyes. If there was a time for divine intervention it was now. But nothing happened.

Euan knew about her son, he just didn't know that Billy Dawson was the father.

"He's my son," she said simply.

Billy took a few seconds to absorb what Annie had just said.

"But, Ian's your son, yours and Euan's and Lexie's your daughter," he was on his feet now and moving towards Annie, "so if he's your son, then who is his father?"

He turned her around to face him. Annie said nothing, but she may as well have screamed it from the rooftops.

The realisation dawned on Billy as he remembered his encounter with John Adams and how he'd felt he'd known him in the past. The connection was now plain.

"He's mine?" he whispered.

Annie nodded. It was out at last.

"But how, when...?" Billy felt he'd been hit by a sledgehammer.

"It was that time down by the river," Annie said quietly, "during the flax gathering. After you left me and went to Scotland and married Mary, John was born in the poorhouse in Belfast and adopted by Dr Adams and his wife."

"Does Euan know about this?" he asked.

"He knows that John's my son, yes, but he doesn't know that you're his father. And he won't know Billy, not ever," she added vehemently.

"He's our son," Billy breathed, tears forming in his eyes. "All this time and I never knew."

Annie sat down again, spent of energy and weak with relief that Billy, at last, knew the truth.

"So, you see Billy," Annie said gently, "Sarah and John are both your children, that's why they must be apart now and forever."

Billy grasped her hands in his. "And where does this leave us Annie," he asked, urgently, "me and you?"

Annie pulled her hands from his.

"It leaves us nowhere, Billy," she said, "there is no me and you anymore."

"There's you and Josie and your daughters and me and Euan and my children and that's how it's going to stay."

Billy felt a chill round his heart. "You don't mean that Annie," he said, "I mean really mean it?"

"Go home, Billy," she told him, calmly, "to Josie. When John returns to Ireland, I'll let you know his address and if you want to write to him and let him know you're his father, then so be it, but he won't hear it from me."

"I have a son," he kept repeating, "and Annie Pepper is his mother."

Annie braced herself. Here was the man she had loved for so long, but it was all now too late. Too much water had passed under the bridge for both of them.

"Thank you Annie," Billy said as he turned to leave, "for loving me and forgiving me for the hurt I must have caused you, but most of all Annie, thank you for giving me a fine son."

She heard the door close and his footsteps fade as he walked out of her life for the last time. Calmly and without any more guilt or fear, she looked at the clock. Ian would be home from school soon and Lexie home from work, but most of all Euan would be coming home, at six as usual and she knew he'd always come home to her every day, for the rest of their lives.